The Night's Fable
©2022, Ochoie

All rights reserved. This book or any portion thereof may not be reproduced or used in any manner whatsoever without the express written permission of the publisher except for the use of brief quotations in a book review.

The Night's Fable

In Urban Prose

OCHOIE

Greg and family,
Thank you for
reading.
- Ophoie

The Good Night

Without a stitch, hitch, hiccup, or the tiniest glitch, Night swung over the mortal world as he always did – sowing his goodwill through his darkness. Out of all the Nights that reigned before him, he was a Good Night and felt it was important to spread goodness on Earth since darkness had a certain stigma, a mark, a *je ne sais quoi* of being, well… rather dark. So it was his mission to show the world that darkness didn't have to lack light — it didn't have to be so gloomy or even worse — scary. *Darkness is goodness!* he would say, and by those words, he reigned.

At every nocturnal hour's performance, once Dusk gave his cue, he tickled the stars until they laughed with brightness, then gallantly danced with the Moon Mother until she radiated full of joy. Once the stardust settled from his first and second act, he would become still and strum his guitar that spread tranquility on Earth, making dreams sweet with lullabies.

This act was his goodwill to the world, and he never tired of it. Nor did his court and after every performance, applause and shouts of *Bravo!* So tall he stood, head and chest raised high from the overflow of ovations. But it was the praise that rippled from humans that he found to be most rewarding. So for his final act and encore, rather than taking a bow, Night would lay his ear down onto the world and count how many times he heard the praises of *Good Night*.

His ears rang proudly as he heard, "Good Night, mom!" "Good Night, dad!" "Good Night, sir!" "Good Night, madam!" "Good Night, dog!" "Good Night, cat!" "Good Night, Good Night, Good Night!" was said all around the world, in different languages, and he counted every one.

His court, which consisted of Gods, Goddesses, and Mystical Forces, found the act of the count to be a bit peculiar, but to appease him, every dinner at court, someone would always ask, "What was the count this time, Night?"

He would always smugly reply, "Somewhere in the billions."

"Goodness Darkness! That's quite high."

To appease him even further, a God or Goddess would ask, "But what was the exact count, Night?"

The count always varied in the slightest of numbers, but it was always a count he was happy to report and this particular court dinner, just before he was about to cut into his pie, he noted, "It was 6, 415, 218, 000."

"My! That's almost the entire population."

This banter always followed with Night making a toast. "It shows that our reign is strong. Darkness is Goodness!"

Goblets would clink and the court would continue to toast, "To the Good Night!"

His goodness even attracted the love of the queen, the Sun.

To tease her in passing, he would brag, "My count was 6, 415, 218, 000, yours?"

She found the count silly and would giggle as she said, "I rule by the goodness of faith, my love, and not by the count."

One might have seen this union of love cursed and star-crossed as they both were opposing rulers, complete opposites with different work schedules. Still, the two shared an unbreakable bond that made them the most successful rulers.

"When you fall, I rise, my love," the Sun would say.

The Night would kiss her hand with deep affection, "Until the end of time, my queen."

The Divine Clock supporting this union allowed the two rulers to come together during every eclipse, including the Sun's Jubilee, the popular event of the season.

Gossip always searched for the infamous couple during the Jubilee ceremony, hoping to catch them in an act that would expose their relationship. But to dispel Gossip and unwarranted attention, both sat openly, side by side, on each other's throne.

At the end of the celebration, Night would bow to the Sun and ask her on a date. Even though the two rulers were certain to reunite for the next eclipse, the gesture made the Sun swoon.

"My queen, it has been so lovely to see you again. May you accompany me for the next eclipse?" the Night would always ask.

The crowds would gush as they loved seeing such a display of affection from their rulers.

The Sun would gracefully rise and say the words the Night always longed to hear, "Good Night, my love, until the next eclipse."

Hearing the praise of *Good Night* coming from his love, the Sun, warmed his hue to the deepest of royal blues. He was such a happy and Good Night that he spread his goodness on Earth time and time again.

Until, the Night got sick with a mysterious cold and became bedridden, nobody knew what caused it, and even though treason was in the back of everyone's mind, someone had to step in to fulfill his duties on Earth. His younger brother and only other sibling, the Darkest Night, who reigned over the Black Nebulous, came rushing to help.

The Darkest Night whispered in his brother's ear, "Brother, it would be such an honor to stand in for you while you focus on getting well."

The Night quickly propped himself up at the suggestion, "Nonsense! I can still tend to my duties." But when he attempted to get out of bed, he was struck with a dizzy spell.

His right hand in command, The Greatest Wind, aided him back to bed as the Night was too unwell to lay his darkness onto Earth.

The Darkest Night pleaded with his brother to let him help, "I know I rule by a different hand, but I can rule under your order and do just as you do. After all, what choice do you have, brother?"

After pondering the thought for a second, he realized his brother was right; who else could lay darkness over Earth but one who is of the night? "Brother, you will do just as I do? Lay your darkness with goodness?"

"Yes, I will play by your rules," agreed the Darkest Night. He was pleased his brother placed faith in him.

"Very well then, please spread your darkness when Dusk gives you the cue," said the Night, relieved he could rest, and all would be well.

Quickly, the Darkest Night stepped in, and when Dusk gave his cue with a wink and a nod, the Darkest Night spread his darkness just as Night did — with goodness. He tickled the stars until they lit up, danced with the Moon Mother until she radiated her light, and strummed his brother's guitar bringing sweet dreams to Earth.

Afterward, the Greatest Wind, Night's top commander, greeted the Darkest Night. "A job well done, sir. Your brother will be pleased. Now for the matter of the count. He has requested for me to report the count of *Good Night*."

"The count? What do you mean by the count?" said the Darkest Night.

"Night is requesting the report of how many times humans have said *Good Night* in the world," said the Greatest Wind.

"This is the most absurd thing I have ever heard. My brother wants me to count how many times the world has sung his praises?" The Darkest Night was annoyed by his brother's ego.

The Greatest Wind reminded him, "You did say you would do just like your brother Night does."

He rolled his eyes, "Fine. I guess I'm off for the count of *Good Nights*."

So the Darkest Night laid his ear on the world, just as his brother did, and counted the praise of *Good Night*. He didn't understand the significance of the count and became agitated every time he had to do it. He mocked: *How easy it is to bestow goodness on Earth! And to think, I thought this job would be challenging.*

Days became an entire week, and Darkest Night was bored with the same routine at every nocturnal hour. *There has to be room for improvisation*, he thought. *Maybe I can do just as my brother does, but in my own way.* The thought of reigning with his darkness brought him excitement. So when Dusk gave his cue, rather than tickle the stars to twinkle with bright light, he shook them until they shot out of the sky. Rather than waltz with the Moon Mother, he swung her high and low, making her exhausted and only half-lit. Instead of strumming his brother's guitar, he plugged it into the cosmos and blared his songs of meteor rocks. It felt good to let loose and be himself, and he continued to do it.

The act disrupted Earth. The people began to have nightmares, a crime wave spiked, and everyone began to fear the dark. Unaware that he was shifting the scales and causing havoc on Earth, when the Darkest Night laid his ear down onto the world for the count, to his surprise, it was pretty low. *Oh no! My dear brother will be displeased* — he at first thought.

But as he continued to listen for the count of *Good Night*, he heard a different kind of praise. Disgruntled voices shouted, "Darkest Night!" "A Dark Night to you, sir!" "A Dark Night to you, madam!" "Darkest Night, unstill night!" "Darkest, Darkest, Darkest Night!" was said worldwide.

Stunned to hear such recognition, he murmured, "I'm liked?... I'm liked?" Then he began to parade and dance. "I'm liked! I'm liked! How wonderful to be liked. Darkness is darkness!" He shouted with certainty and continued to turn each 'good' night into the 'darkest.'

When Night fully recovered from the mystery illness and could stand tall again, he thanked his brother with a court celebration in his honor.

During the court dinner, the Night toasted, "To my brother! Despite his difference in ruling hand, the Darkest Night kept Earth dark with goodness. Darkness is goodness!"

"Hear, hear!" Toasted the court, unaware of how the scales had shifted on Earth.

Gossip rose from her seat and addressed the Darkest Night to start a bit of controversy. "Your dark grace, how many counts of *Good Night* are you departing with?"

The Darkest Night turned to his brother and addressed the court. "I am pleased to report that a new praise has developed in my brother's absence, and two different counts are rippling in from the human world."

The dinner hall clamored at the news, "Nonsense!" "Did he say there are two counts now?" "How dare he!"

Confused by the matter, the Night put down his goblet and asked, "What do you mean by two counts?"

Smugly, the Darkest Night rolled his finger in buttercream pie for a taste and said, "Well… it seems I have developed a following… but don't worry dear brother, many still sing your praises."

Upset, Night shouted, "What is the count of *Good Night*?"

Shocked seeing the Night lose his temper, the court of Gods, Goddesses, and mystical forces became still and silent.

To reassure his brother of his praise, the Darkest Night replied, "Don't worry, brother, your count remains high in the hundreds."

Night fumed with stardust, "In the hundreds! What have you done?"

"Brother, I don't mean to brag. After all, the count was a duty you passed down to me, but the praise of the Darkest Night is in the millions."

Stricken by rage, the Night became tongue-tied and rose tall. He pointed to the Black Nebulous but could only muster up a few words. "Go! Leave at once."

Saddened by his brother's reaction, the Darkest Night grabbed his coat. "Brother, I wish you could see that this is what true darkness is supposed to be. Why try and fight it? Darkness is darkness."

The Night didn't hear his brother. He could only think about the low count. Trying to keep his composure and stay positive, he reassured the court: "I'll be stronger with my goodwill. We will all be stronger from this!"

So when Dusk gave his cue, he eagerly swung over the world with overflowing amounts of cheer. The stars beamed brightly again, so happy to see the Good Night. The Moon Mother twirled joyfully at his side, and the strums of his guitar cut through the thick darkness that loomed over the world, making dreams sweet once more.

Afterward, he listened for the count, hoping he had restored harmony on earth, but something unusual happened. Rather than hear the words and praise of *Good Night,* he listened to a loud thumping sound that went on and on and got louder and louder. *What's this I hear?* The noise disturbed him.

At first, Night dismissed the sound, thinking something was wrong with his ears. *It must be stardust,* he thought. So he went to the realm's physician, and his ears were crystal clear of any stardust residue.

Thinking all was fine and well, Night laid his ear down for the count but only heard thumping and clanking. *Why that sound is of a Heartbeat!* he figured. *How unusual that I can pick up on such a thing.* He simply dismissed the occurrence as interference from some sort of satellite frequency.

But just as he was about to swing his darkness over the east coast city of New York, the sound of the Heartbeat clunked so loudly it interrupted Night's composed, perfectly timed performance. Aggravated by the nuisance of the irregular Heartbeat, Night began his search for it.

He scoured the city with his crystal telescopic lens that could look through any nook and cranny of the human world. But unfortunately, the telescope led him on a wild chase, unable to search for something that couldn't be seen.

Being so strong, this Heartbeat has to come from an Olympian, one of athletic strength. So the telescope scoured for every top athlete, searching for the best and victorious in their sport. But none matched the Heartbeat that clunked so loudly.

Perhaps, this Heartbeat is coming from a place closer to the heavens that can echo through the sky. So the telescope searched for the Heartbeat in the highest skyscrapers, yet nothing. The Heartbeat remained undetected.

As time went on, even though it was hard to do, he gave up searching for the elusive Heartbeat. The Night became faced with another nuisance — his brother. The Darkest Night continued to linger over the world and spread his darkness. The Night feared his brother would want to continue to build his following and take over his reign. To avoid this, he needed to take precautions and set a plan.

The Night decided to find his chosen one, a human, a hero, that could restore harmony from the flipside — Earth. This hero would be his insurance if a takeover occurred. So the search for his hero on Earth began, but every time he peered down his magical telescope to seek out his perfect hero, the Heartbeat, like a noisy, banging construction site, would disrupt his focus.

Frustrated, Night lost his grace and struck the sky and shook the stars, which got the attention of the Moon Mother and counselor of all.

"My son, it is unlike you to lose your temper. What has you so disturbed?"

"I can't find what I seek, and I must find one before I can begin to find the other," said the Night, holding back his temper.

"What is it that you seek? Maybe I can help you," said the Moon Mother in her calm voice.

The Night took a deep breath as he tried to calm himself. "I need to find the chosen one, but there is a disturbance, and I can't seem to think clearly."

"I see… Well, finding the chosen one is quite the task. You should enlist the help of the Goddess Desire."

Interrupting the Moon, he shouted, "She's a nomad! A vagabond! She has defied and rebelled against the rules of the Mystical Realm. How can I trust her?"

The Moon Mother and protector of the planet, who sees the good in all, said, "Don't be so quick to judge my son. She is no longer a child and has already done your work for you on Earth with her gift of whispers. She does stand for goodness, and it is time you work with her."

"I will take your counsel under consideration, mother. Until then, I will look for the chosen one on my own. If I could only make that disturbing Heartbeat disappear!"

"Maybe, you will find what you seek within your darkness, and while your stillness grows, what you seek might come to you." Thus the Moon Mother wisely advised.

Embarrassed by his temperament, he took the Moon's advice and became silent and still. He closed his eyes and looked within his darkness. Sure enough, the pesky Heartbeat came crashing through with its cymbals. This time, rather than get annoyed, Night listened to it.

In a state of complete darkness, the Heartbeat visually came alive and no longer was just a beat, but a heart that grew feet and raced fast. It took him straight to the human city streets. *Ah, the Belly of New York*, he thought as he recognized the area. The Heartbeat gained speed, jumped over a railing, stumbled down steps, and just as a metro train came crashing into view, the Heartbeat stopped and led Night to somewhere unlikely, somewhere Night's telescope would have never led him to. Then the Heartbeat revealed to him an unlikely soul, one Night and his telescope would have overlooked. As this soul slept, the Heartbeat spoke to Night, "Take a peek. In this body lies the strong heart of the one you seek."

"Oh, my bright stars!" Night jumped from his seat.

He quickly sought counsel from the Moon. "Mother, I did as you said and became still and looked within my darkness, and the chosen one was revealed to me by the very same Heartbeat that I found to be a nuisance."

The Moon Mother, glad to have been of service, said, "That is a wonderful Night. Now, you can easily strike the world again with your mind at ease."

"Oh, but there is one thing that puzzles me, so I seek your counsel." The Night took a deep breath, "The chosen one revealed to me is not a human, but a creature, a soul doubtful to possess the qualities of a hero. Therefore, I fear my judgment is misleading me."

"I see, then tell me about this creature, my son," said the Moon Mother in her serene tone.

"Well, it's nocturnal and knows darkness, which is good. But I find it disturbing that it sees darkness as a curse because it has experienced darkness from the depths and foulest parts of the Earth. This creature doesn't know that darkness is goodness! How can the Heartbeat lead me to this soul?"

"My dear son, maybe that's how you will restore your reign by overseeing the most unlikely event from the most unlikely soul. And simply by this event alone, it can overturn any darkness to goodness from the bottom up."

"From the bottom up, from the bottom up." The Night kept repeating to himself. "I like the sound of that. It brings me peace that such an event can echo from the depths of Earth."

The Night thanked the Moon Mother and walked away, restored with something he had been missing for a while — faith. He knew what needed to be done and no longer sought interest in the count but focused on what he enjoyed the most — making every performance on Earth a *Good Night.*

Night and The Greatest Wind

Night called for his right hand and top commander, the Greatest Wind, and handed him his telescope. The Greatest Wind was titled the Greatest by merit alone. Seas feared him, the Lands braced themselves before his landfall and the Skies parted as no other wind had flown so high in altitude, surpassing the stars. Night, humbled by the Greatest Wind's servitude and loyalty throughout his reign, saw him as a son and knew he could count on him.

Night pointed down from the noctilucent clouds. "That one, you must go to that one."

The Greatest Wind trained his gaze down Night's telescope, which led his sights down a funnel of far-reaching magnification from Night's sky to a grim, trash-filled alley. "Sire, I don't see a thing but pitch darkness and grime."

"Then you are not looking, my son."

The Greatest Wind deepened his focus through the crystal lens when the silhouette of Night's chosen one emerged. The Greatest Wind gasped. "Sire, my eyes must be mistaken. What I see is not human. It's a..."

"Your eyes do not deceive you. That is indeed my chosen one."

"Sire, this is a very unusual request. Pardon me for wanting to know, why is your choice not of a human soul? But rather this foul creature."

The Night grew more prominent as he looked down at the Greatest Wind. "You are becoming very tiresome and small with your judgment, is the task too difficult for you?"

"No, sire, no order is too tall or, in this case, rather small. I'll send my top-ranking Low Winds to gather a whisper from the Goddess Desire."

Being so broad and almighty, Night had no direct influence over human souls, making the Goddess of Desire's whispers essential even if he didn't want to admit it. Through the power of her whisper, he could instill his goodwill, which would come in handy if a takeover ever were to occur.

"Not this time; I need you to gather and deliver the whisper yourself. I hear the Goddess Desire has relocated once again, and my telescope has not been able to detect her new portal of residence. You are the only one that can find her quickly and trace her location," said Night as he began to pace back and forth. "I don't understand why she has chosen this life for herself, living amongst humans like a vagabond. She is a Goddess! For heaven's sake!" Frustrated, Night went into an unusual coughing frenzy.

Alarmed by Night's state of health, the Greatest Wind pleaded, "Sire, my duties are of greater importance here by your side. You are still recovering from this mystery illness. Surely I can oversee the order while investigating how this illness occurred."

"My brother is causing this illness! He is still casting his darkness on Earth, making it harder for me to fulfill my duties. Therefore, it is of greater importance for this whisper to be delivered rapidly and for no one to know to whom it is going other than the Goddess Desire. Understood?"

The Greatest Wind bowed to Night and dutifully replied, "Understood."

The Night grew tall and cast his shadow onto the Greatest Wind. "I almost don't see you anymore with all your slogging around. You must go now or stay unseen from me for all eternity."

"Yes, sire, I'll leave at once," said the Greatest Wind, dropping at a ferocious speed.

It was in the Greatest Wind's will to protect and serve Night for eternity, but in this particular dark hour, as Night's heavens were casting a shadow from above, he found himself in conflict with carrying out Night's order. Not only was he unsure about Night's chosen one, but he would have to seek the Goddess Desire.

It had felt like another lifetime since he had been in her presence. He was just a Northern Wind without a title when they met. It pained him to think of their sordid past. The thought of seeing her again made the wind nervous. And for a cold, unwavering Greatest Wind of the North, it upset him to feel as such. Having Feelings was a trait no other wind had come to possess, and he found it to be a weakness. So his ferocity became wicked to the wisp and bad to the billow to overcome such a trait.

He vowed in times past that he would never see her again. *It's better off that way,* he figured. But here he was on Night's orders heading earthbound to seek the Goddess Desire and gather a whisper from her. *At least I know how to find her. The Night was undoubtedly right about that.* But to do that, he would have to do some digging and exhume his past, which was something he wasn't ready to do.

He took a deep breath and inhaled the heavenly Northern air before heading earthbound towards the southern lands, where he first met the Goddess of Desire. Then, like a cold shot, he guzzled the icy breeze. Its chill, brittleness, and piercing sting traveled through him and gave him the bitter strength for a crash landing.

The Goddess Desire and The Belly

Born of fire, the Goddess of Desire ignited every soul that received her whispers. It was her sense of duty and her own goodwill to empower those who would create positive change and make their dreams come true.

Unlike the rest of Night's court, she resided on Earth, where she lived amongst her subjects, humans, to study them and learn their deepest longings. Night thought her nomadic lifestyle to be rebellious and wild, lacking the grace of a true goddess. But on the contrary, the Goddess of Desire prided herself on being a nomad and couldn't bear to think of residing in Night's stuffy court. Instead, she found it more fascinating to be in constant movement with an ever-changing world.

So by the game of chance, she spun her Earth globe to dictate her portal residence, wherever her finger would land. She moved where the winds blew high and low, where lands were evergreen, and where countries bloomed in color.

Yet, in all her previous residences, she hadn't experienced living in a big metropolitan city and, even more so, its bustling Belly. So when she spun her globe and her finger landed on the Belly of New York, she wondered what chance had in store. So she packed up her court and, with a twist of a key, moved her portal once more.

After a long day of moving, the Goddess of Desire took a break and circled the city streets swirling in the excitement of the newness. *The Belly of New York! Finally, finally, I've made it!* But, unlike New York's heart or the sum of its parts, the Belly roared with artistic musing. Filled with actors, artists, musicians, and all who hungered to make their dreams come true — the Goddess of Desire couldn't help but think, *This is my city!*

Beauty and Vice had various storefronts selling wares on every street corner, tempting humans to change their fates. *Buy this Bag to Brag, Wear this Shoe to Woo, A Scent to Tempt, Try this beauty potion to get Love into motion,* and other lurings cascaded throughout the storefronts.

"My! This city's core is certainly not for those seeking solace," said Violet, the Goddess's lady in waiting.

Violet, an esteemed swirl of smoke, born from the Moon's crater, was the Goddess's gatekeeper and a most loyal lady in waiting.

Both strolled the New York Belly streets, shapeshifted into human form, the Goddess of Desire as a classy gentleman and Violet, trying to fit in local hipster attire.

"What's that swishing noise, Violet?" said the Goddess of Desire as she looked behind her, trying to locate the noise.

"It's my pants, my lady. They are quite oddly fitting. *Faux leather,* they are. The salesperson assured me they were in style for this area. But I haven't felt this uncomfortable since the corset days. So I think I will shapeshift back to my smoke form and remain unseen."

"I think you just need some wiggle room, Violet. Besides, the point is to be seen!"

She tipped her hat, greeting the locals.

"Yes, my lady, and you are doing a good job at that. Everyone is looking at you, and might I add that you look very handsome in that tailcoat suit. What sparked such a shapeshift?"

"Well, I thought I would put on the Ritz as I imagined New York would be, but now that I'm looking around…." The Goddess noticed the locals wearing ripped-up denim and rock tees, "I think I got confused with the time period. But, nevertheless, we need to make friends and ignite this city."

"Yes, your grace," said Violet, just as a tincture shop caught her attention. "Oh, my lady, we need tincture and tea for your whisper cupboard. Let's start there!"

Distracted by a whimsically designed pastry shop in the shape of a cloud, the Goddess of Desire replied, "You go ahead, Violet. That patisserie is calling my name."

"Oh yes, my lady, that sounds splendid. I will meet you after." Violet swished away, heading towards the tincture shop.

The Goddess Desire couldn't help to feel a bit of *déjà vu* when she caught a whiff of the macarons from Claude's Patisserie. *Interesting, it doesn't smell like earthbound spices,* she suspiciously sniffed. Then she noticed a distinct coiled curl bouncing off the macaron maker's forehead. She quickly realized it was Claude the Cloud, pastry chef of Night's court, sampling his macarons.

"A *Fluffy Cloud* to send you drifting?" Claude handed a patron a macaron.

"Claude! Is that you?" the Goddess said in a low secretive voice.

Claude, unable to recognize the Goddess, replied, "Hello sir, quite the exquisite suit. I haven't seen a tailcoat suit that exquisite since the Victorian era!" He coughed as he realized it was the 21st century and quickly corrected himself. "I mean, since Halloween... any morsel to tempt the sweet tooth today?"

The Goddess of Desire giggled, remembering she wasn't in her Goddess form. Then, she leaned in and said, "Claude, it's me, the Goddess Desire."

Confused, Claude observed the tall gentleman up and down, and when he met the man's eyes, he recognized the flames and amber of none other than the Goddess of Desire. He floated over the counter, stirring in excitement, and greeted her with a kiss on the cheek. "Goddess of Fire and Flame before my eyes! My dear, where have you been? It has been such a long time. You were a little spitfire the last time I saw you, and look at you now!"

The Goddess began to blush as they got the attention of onlooking patrons waiting to get their macarons, and in a low whispering voice, she said, "Claude, what on earth are you doing here? I never pegged you for an earthbound cloud."

"My dear, you didn't hear? Gossip had its way with this news. It circulated all through Night's court. I was expelled, vanished, poofed from the court."

"What, not you, Claude! What happened?"

"According to Night's order, I dabbled into the darker arts of pastry making. I don't understand it. I simply whipped up a soufflé of a wondrous spell, and allegedly it made Night and his court gold and yellow as the sun."

The Goddess laughed, "I wish I were there to have seen it, Claude, but I'm sorry you were cast out."

"Night cast me out immediately. I do miss my position in court, but I am now labeled Fallen. Like you, I suppose." Then changed the subject, "What are you doing here? In the Belly, my dear."

The Goddess didn't like to be referred to as Fallen; she had been called many things by the Night's court, but Fallen was by far the worst.

Seeing he struck a nerve, Claude grabbed the tall gent of a Goddess by the hand and led her to his tiered display of cloud-filled macarons in the most decadent variety, "My dear, you must try some of my specialty sweets."

Remembering how much she loved Claude's concoctions of sweets, she plopped herself on the counter stool and, with delight, said, "Claude, I trust your judgment. Which splendid macarons shall I taste first?"

Claude became excited to serve someone from the court again. "Goddess, you just sit and let me bring you my special macarons from the back."

Claude clapped to get the attention of Austin, his newest pastry chef, a local Belly hipster who stood confused, trying to make out the odd spices in Claude's kitchen.

"Austin, can I trouble you for some assistance?" called Claude.

Austin clumsily walked over as Claude formally introduced him to the Goddess Desire, who sat on a high bar stool with her coattail hanging.

Aloof to mystical royalty, Austin shrugged his shoulders and greeted the Goddess. "Okay, sure, hi."

Embarrassed by his chef's manners, Claude said, "Austin, please bring the Goddess a tray of *Flaming Fire* macarons. The ones I asked you to make earlier."

Austin replied tepidly, "Oh, I thought you were joking. So you really wanted me to make that?"

Claude nearly choked on his puff of breath, not having a *Flaming Fire* macaron for the Goddess of Desire. "Assistants these days!" He quipped, wiping his brow of sweat beads. "I have something special, though, something I whipped up myself. Indulge in the macarons from the serving tray, my dear, while I fetch it."

The Goddess Desire was perfectly fine devouring the macarons available. She first tried *Stardust Rose*, which made her face sparkle like diamonds, then stuffed herself with *Fluffy Cloud*, causing her to levitate off her stool. Then, just as she was about to try *Gooey Dark Night*, Claude came out with one single macaron on a tray.

The Goddess's eyes brightened at the sight of the well-crafted macaron. "It looks lovely, Claude. What is this?"

He proudly announced, "This, my dear, is Nostalgia. It transcends time. It is perfect for you. It will bring back feelings of youth and play."

The Goddess carefully grabbed what seemed to be a simple macaron in proportion and pale color but sprouted with sprinkles of memory-inducing thyme when examined closely. She took a whiff and could smell the warm breeze of a Texas night. Quickly engulfing it, thyme burst like pop rocks, swirling in her mouth with sweet memories of her youth.

But just as the macaron began to settle, it became bitter. Rather than spring with joyful memories, the Nostalgia macaron brought about a painful one – a memory she had hoped she had suppressed. "I don't think this one's for me, Claud. How long will this last? I'm feeling quite ill."

Claude began to panic as he thought, *Oh no! Not again!*

He rummaged through his spices. Everything seemed right until he came across an unmarked spice bottle. "Austin, What's this? Why is this here?"

Austin put on his large rimmed eyeglasses but still found it difficult to make out the strange labeling of the spice. "Yeah, dunno, isn't that nutmeg?"

"Are you absurd! I don't carry such a simple uncomplex spice as nutmeg. Where did you get this spice from?" Claude exclaimed in a panic.

Austin pointed to the cabinet that was marked VERY POTENT.

No, No, No! Claude thought as he opened the spice cabinet and noticed one of his most potent spellbound spices was missing. He nervously walked over to the Goddess. "My dear, don't be alarmed. But you might be in a state of Nostalgia for about… Let's say a week or so."

"A week of Nostalgia!" The Goddess of Desire panted, nearly shape-shifting back to her true form. "No! No! No!" She cried. Nearly falling over her stool and tripping on the tails of her coat — her fire began to emerge. "'I've gotta go!" Quickly fleeing the shop.

Claude called out to the Goddess, advising her, "Think of a better past! My dear."

The Goddess sprinted towards her portal and tried to think of more joyous times, but the spell of Nostalgia kept taking her to her worst memory. She turned onto a cobbled alley where her portal became visible and burst into flames just as she lept through. Then headed straight to Moon's Garden, where she fell on the foot of her favorite orchids and began to cry.

The Moon Mother, with her nurturing light, consoled the Goddess. "My dear, you have come here many times to cry. It is time to confront what you have buried deep in your heart. You have to let go of this pain."

The Goddess wiped her tears as she spoke. "It is Love that pains me. I reign with Desire and I should have known better than to put my heart above my fire."

"My dearest Desire, you need Love to fan the fire. It is not wrong to hold Love in your heart and reign with Desire. But, you need to confront what pains you. I must warn you. He is coming. Whether you like it or not, the Greatest Wind is coming to see you. It's best to settle this now or be burdened by the shackles of your past." Advised the Moon.

The Goddess Desire calmed herself in thought. In truth, the Goddess could sense the Greatest Wind was near even before she walked into Claude's shop. She smelled him when she took a bite of Nostalgia. But, unfortunately, the macaron only brought it to the surface, and now the time she dreaded and secretly waited for was coming to her.

The Goddess Desire looked up to the Moon and asked, "Can I ever forgive him?"

The Moon Mother replied, "You must. It's the only way to move forward — with Love. You've held on too long. It's time to fulfill your purpose and show Night's court the Goddess you have always been."

The Goddess curtsied to the Moon and let her flames span out into wings. "Yes, I am ready, and the Greatest Wind is about to meet who I have become."

The Moon pleaded: "Desire, you must let him go with Love."

The Goddess stubbornly looked back at the Moon. "I know of no love. I only know of fire."

The Wicked Wind Returns

With grumbling fury, the Greatest Wind took the rural Texas town of Shiner by surprise when he broke landfall. He watched with enjoyment while its residents ran for cover.

"Ha!" He snickered, remembering what his strength felt like to hit the dirt again.

The fluorescence of a pink neon moon sign flickered, fighting against the blows of his unforgiving winds. It called to him as it buzzed with the lingering traces of the Goddess of Desire's electricity and the chord of a sliding guitar. It was there, *Desirée's Tavern*, a speakeasy of a saloon where the Goddess of Desire once held her portal residence.

It was all coming back to him, just as he remembered it to be, and it had remained the same as if he had never left. He inhaled the moist Texas air that calmed his billows in its warmth and headed to the saloon where it all began.

The Greatest Wind walked in and shapeshifted himself into the same human form he always shapeshifted into — a cowboy — wearing black from head to toe. The only color that emanated from him was his piercing blue eyes.

"Well-well-well, look what the storm dragged in? Hello, my friend, it's been a while," said the barkeep.

"Hello Charlie, it's good to see you again," said the Greatest Wind as he looked around for the Goddess's portal.

"What's your pleasure? What can I getcha?"

The Greatest Wind settled himself at the bar. "I'll have my usual Charlie if you can remember that far back."

Charlie poured a glass of the strongest Storm Steep he had. "Here you go, my friend. Your usual, nice and neat for the Greatest Wind."

The Greatest Wind slung it back and asked for another as he continued to look around, wondering if her portal remained there.

"What brings you back to these parts?" Charlie asked.

The Greatest Wind slammed the empty glass on the bar, signaling for a refill. "Duty."

Charlie raised a pint glass and toasted, "Ah, Duty!"

The Storm Steep was more potent than he remembered, which woke his lingering wisp that began to fiddle with the piano keys. He peeked inside its casing to see if it was there.

Charlie suspiciously asked, "Whatcha looking for, friend?"

"You know what I'm looking for, and I must find it — friend." Dryly said the Greatest Wind.

"It's out of commission. You best find Miss Violet if you are looking for business matters with the Goddess Desire."

The Greatest Wind had no patience for words. He had no patience to figure out if Charlie was a friend or foe and brazenly leaped over the bar, grabbing Charlie by the throat. "Where is it, Charlie? Or I will tear this place to shreds."

"Like you did before? We will rebuild again, my friend, but if you hurt her, you will tip the scales, and this time for eternity, and we can't have that happen."

The Greatest Wind let go of Charlie. "It's not my intention to tip the scales or hurt her. It never has been. Whatever happened between the

Goddess and I is in the past. I just need to find her, Charlie. I would let her be if it wasn't for Night's order. I know she's better off that way."

Despite his temper, Charlie knew the Greatest Wind was a dutiful and loyal servant to Night, so after a second of mulling it over, he straightened his collar and said, "Follow me."

Charlie walked behind the bar towards a paneled wall and unlocked a portal with a unique knocking sequence. The wall opened like an airtight jar, releasing the preservative of cigar smoke, country music, and the chatter of southern mystics.

The Greatest Wind continued to follow Charlie through the crowd of patrons as they wondered why he was there.

"Is that the Greatest Wind?"

"What's he doing in these parts?"

"Storm alert! I better tend to my farm!"

Charlie led him back into an old hangar that housed large crates and barrels of mead and steep.

"I've never seen this before, Charlie. Is this a new addition?"

"Nope, it's always been here. It's where we brew. I made sure to keep you and the Goddess out. To think of the trouble you guys could have caused here!" Charlie led the Greatest Wind past the brewery.

"Different times, Charlie. Those were different times," chuckled the Greatest Wind.

"Alright, there it is. Good luck. You're gonna need it." Charlie pointed to the corner of the room.

There, cloaked in a tapestry secured with red tape that read, *Enter At Your Own Risk,* was the Goddess's secret portal – her mystic music box, Maestro.

Maestro was given to the Goddess as a gift from Night while preparing for her coronation. He thought it would help her study better, but Maestro wasn't just any music box. Instead, it was a Warper gadget that could compose memory and time from music.

Maestro carried thousands of the Goddesses' vinyl memories, but there was one song that she inserted for the Greatest Wind if he ever needed to find her. It would lead him straight to her, wherever she may be in the present time.

He wheezed at the sight of the dusty spider-webbed Maestro that once was lit with bright atomic lights and played the music of his youth in the wild. "I'll have another shot of that Storm Steep, Charlie."

"Sure thing, I'll bring you two."

"Good man, thank you," said the Greatest Wind, about to plug Maestro into the socket.

Charlie turned back to warn the Greatest Wind. "Easy there, don't be so quick to start that thing. It took on a life of its own when the Goddess of Desire left it behind. Some mystics went missing playing her songs. Some say they are stuck in the past, unable to break free to the present."

"I'll take my chances," said the Greatest Wind as he grabbed his steep and slung it back. He plugged in Maestro, and with a nudge, it lit up, swinging its arms uncontrollably.

The Greatest Wind grinned while he rummaged through the various vinyl recollections that swung like pages of a history book. "Nice to see you again, Maestro. Now, where is it? Where is the song?"

He sifted through each song while flashbacks of her warm embrace flooded in. Then he came to it — their song that blinked *Ready for Play*.

The song was the gateway to the Goddess Desire's present portal in time, and even though he debated whether to seek out Violet, her gatekeeper, he secretly wanted to listen to their song one last time. Besides, the easy way was never the path for someone titled The Greatest Wind.

A gold coin flew out of Maestro's mouth and circled the floor in figure eight, landing with heads facing up. He grabbed another shot of the cloudy steep and slipped the coin into its slot. "I'm ready," said the Greatest Wind anxiously. He pressed the song selection and sat back.

Maestro plucked its needle and, like a grand conductor, waved its hand over the vinyl 45, setting the tempo of time, spinning its wheel — counterclockwise. Maestro's atomic lights began to streak and swivel to every curvature on the fast-spinning vinyl. The Greatest Wind braced himself while his winds suctioned into a vacuuming vortex of a song capsule — their song capsule. It crackled out of the worn-out speaker like the flickering flames of the Goddess of Desire. With every starry key that overlapped the warping chorus — the Greatest Wind tumbled backward, rewinding and looping to a time when he was a mere Northern Wind who collided with a soon-to-be anointed Goddess.

Desiree and the Northern Wind

It was the summer moon before the Goddess of Desire's coronation. Typically a Goddess would use this time to prepare and learn about her reign and the traditions of the Mystical Realm, but the young Goddess wanted to roam freely and explore Earth to test her particular skill — her whisper. So, she blindly pointed to a random spot on her globe, which led her finger to the southern lands of Texas. *What better place to test my whispers than on the wild galloping winds of Texas?* She thought. So, without telling Night or the court, she fled.

The Northern Wind descended from Earth's highest peak, and his reputation preceded him everywhere he traveled. He was dangerous by the lands and feared by the ethereal sea, making him a top recruit for Night's Army. But before getting drafted, the Northern Wind wanted one last adventure sweeping over the Americas before entering Night's Army. So he flew off course and headed south.

When the soon-to-be Goddess of Desire collided with the soon-to-be Greatest Wind, the collision left the Texas sky blood orange. It was a disastrous match, to begin with — fire and ice — earth wind and fire — hot and cold — they represented all the clichés of a mismatch, yet they became inseparable.

One evening, after planting whispers in the ears of cowboys and cowgirls, the soon-to-be Goddess announced, "I wrote a letter to Night today, I told him I had changed my name to Desiree, and I will not return for my coronation. So you shall now address me and bow down to your goddess, Desiree, the outlaw."

"Did you also let the heavens know that you would make an excellent Court Jester – Desiree, the outlaw." He teased her.

"Ah, you gust!" She said, throwing her fireballs.

He playfully lunged at her, and both spiraled out of control as they always did when they got too close. However, when Desiree calmed her flames and the Northern Wind kept still, they fell into the perfect embrace — neither too high nor too low but perfectly in flow.

As their love grew through their summer courtship, she wanted to remember it for eternity. So Maestro, her music box, etched every feeling, every loving caress, and every earthly detail of their love onto vinyl. One evening she wanted to present the Northern Wind with a souvenir of their time together.

Desiree tossed a coin up in the air. "Pick a side, heads or tails?"

"Heads, as always." He said as he watched her slam the coin on the saloon table.

"This is your lucky day, heads it is!"

"What are you up to now, Desiree?"

"First, pick a song. Make it worth your while!" She walked to Maestro and inserted the coin, heads first, into its slot.

He didn't mind choosing any particular song, "You're so silly, I don't know, play that one song we both like."

Her finger lingered over the music selection as she hesitated to press it. "Are you sure that's the one you want me to play? It's not very romantic." She sighed.

He grabbed her arm and pulled her closer to him. "That's the one that makes you dance and smile, so yes, play that one."

She nervously pressed the track selection, knowing it would seal their love. "Okay, here we go."

Maestro blared the song throughout the saloon, and the sound of starry keys bounced in a mystic synth.

A patron interrupted them as he yelled, "This isn't country music! What on earth is this?"

She turned to the patron, "Just one minute! It will all be over soon, and we'll get back to saloon tunes. Just give me a minute, please!"

"This music just ain't right." He mumbled.

Another patron added, hovering over his mead, "Kids these days!"

"Thank you!" she yelled to the patrons as she returned her attention to the Northern Wind.

The Northern Wind found the interaction amusing and began to laugh. She always found a way to bring him joy with her brazen fire.

Trying to regain her composure, she anchored her stare into the Northern Wind's deep blue eyes. "This song is a gift to you."

He chuckled, knowing she was up to something sneaky. "What do you mean? A gift?"

"If you ever need to find me in the future, this song will take you to me without a portal key. But first, and this is important to know, you will have to make a pit stop here, right now, at this moment in time, before Maestro transports you and shoots you straight to my gateway, wherever that might be."

The Northern Wind didn't know what to make of her gift; he hadn't thought of their paths or future without each other, and he became moved by the gesture. To avoid showing emotion, he joked and said, "Oh Desiree, I wish you would have revealed this information sooner. I would have chosen a different song."

"You dusty gust!" She said, playfully throwing her fireballs.

He wrapped around her and changed his tone. "All joking aside, thank you, it's a wonderful gift." He kissed her as he began to float, holding her in his arms. "In the future, if I needed to find you, would it change the past... I mean, could it change this exact moment?"

"The past can never become undone. Maestro won't allow that — so we better have a great night tonight." She said, nestling her head into his billows.

"Good." He whirled in her ear. "Because I never want this moment to change. Now, come with me." Leading her out the door.

"What? Where are we going?" Desiree said, looking back at Maestro, that continued to play their song.

"It's my turn. I have a surprise for you." Revving his winds, he devilishly grinned. "Hop on!"

Desiree loved the thrill of adventure, so she jumped right on and held him tightly. Then, like a stampede of wild mustangs, the Northern Wind raced through the vast Texas lands at galloping speeds until he reached a velocity to soar through the skies.

Thrilled by the rush, Desiree yelled, "Higher! Higher!"

"If I take you any higher, we'll wind up in Night's court. Is that where you want to go?" The Northern Wind teased.

"Then lower! lower!" She laughed and exclaimed, "I never want to go back there!"

While racing past the night clouds, Desiree noticed lights of all shapes and sizes coming from the field below. "Is that where we're going?"

"You'll know soon enough. Hang on! We're landing."

If there was one thing the Northern Wind wasn't good at, it was a smooth landing. Truthfully, he had never attempted it. He enjoyed crashing onto land far better. But Desiree was with him, and he had to try.

"Brace yourself, hold tight!" He warned.

But she didn't listen. Instead, she raised her hands that wrestled against the hot summer night's air and yelled with freedom, "Yee-haw!"

The Northern Wind flipped his billows to descend, but his speed was of lightning, and it didn't stop him much. All he could do was extend his billowing feet to catch land, but when they hit the dry ground, he spun out of control. Thrown by the collision, Desiree tumbled, twisted, and rolled down a treacherous hill while the debris of grass and dirt fogged the air.

The Northern Wind quickly shapeshifted back into his teenage human form and stood over the hill. "Are you okay down there?"

Landing flat in a ditch, she couldn't help but irk by his recklessness and said, "Yeah, I guess…."

"Don't move! Let me help you. I'm on my way down."

But when he got to Desiree, she stood dusting herself off. Then snapped at him, "What kind of landing was that?"

He helped her brush the tree branches nestled in her long fiery red hair, but she remained disgruntled. "Now what? Was this your surprise?"

He gently smiled and grabbed her hand. "Trust me. I do have a surprise for you."

Holding one's hand was an intimate gesture in the mystical realm. Most mystics were skilled at reading thoughts by pulse frequency. So to surrender one's hand signified unlocking oneself, having nothing to hide, and sharing vulnerable thoughts with the other.

Giddy by the bold move, Desiree forgot all about the crash and began to decode the Northern Wind's racing pulse while he led her up the steep rocky hill. She picked up on every sensation and thought that ran through him — his embarrassment when he crash-landed — how worried he was when she rolled down the hill — how uncomfortable he felt walking uphill in human denim jeans. But the most reassuring vibration she decoded was that he pulsed with unconditional love.

Unaware that Desiree could pick up on such things, he continued to grip her hand, pulling her up the steepest part of the hill.

"Come on now, Desiree, you're dragging yourself. We're almost there. Just a few more steps to go."

Snapping out of decoding, she began to move swiftly. When they finally reached the top of the hill, a sign shone in the distance and perforated the sky with blinking lights that read — *Texas State Fair*.

When the Northern Wind turned to catch Desiree's reaction, her crystal amber eyes swirled with the reflection of rotating Ferris wheel lights — the *Texas Star*. He smiled as he witnessed the soon-to-be anointed Goddess of Desire reflect beauty from the natural world that he considered mundane.

Awestruck, she asked. "What is this place?"

"I noticed it a few days ago while testing my flight skills. It's supposedly the largest fair in the world. Do you want to go and see what the fuss is about?"

"What are we waiting for?" Desiree said as she began to race the Northern Wind to the entrance.

As soon as they entered the fairgrounds, they became surrounded by spectacle and wonder.

The Texas Pigminster was already in session. Carl, the five-time-winning Berkshire pig, entered the arena. While the other pigs raced through the obstacle course, Carl trotted with his head high, giving a new category for the sport — style.

"I want one! We should get a Carl of our own and have a farm." So said Desiree as she dug her cowboy boots on a stump to take a better look at the happenings.

It warmed the Northern Wind to know that a soon-to-be Goddess would want such a simple life on earth, and for a second, he let himself envision what that life would be.

Amusement rides zizzing and scissoring through the sky got Desiree's attention. "We have to start with that ride!" Desiree pointed to the *Twisting Tornado*, a roller coaster that spiraled upside down and right side up.

The Northern Wind laughed mockingly, "Ha! That's nothing like a tornado, but I'm game."

When they stepped into the cab, the ride conductor pulled the lap bar down to strap them and warned, "Hold tight this thing bucks."

The Greatest Wind grumbled, "I doubt it, but let's give it a whirl."

To emulate the other teenagers in front of them, Desiree snuggled close to the Northern Wind, nervously excited, and said, "Are you ready?"

Not amused by the ride, he joked, "Don't mind me; I'll just be sitting here taking a nap."

Desiree pinched him, "Come on, let's try to pretend we are like them and enjoy the ride."

The ride slowly began to rattle off, picking up speed when The Northern Wind put his arm around her and whispered, "I don't pretend."

She turned to him to see what he meant, and he kissed her passionately. He had never kissed her in such a way, and the combination of his magical smooch with the dizzying rush of the spiraling tornado made her flames emerge and trail like wildfire.

Blood-curdling screams dipped in and out from around them as her fire spiraled out of control. Both remained lip-locked, thinking the screams were coming from the thrill-seekers.

"Fire! Fire!" Ascended from the fairgrounds.

Desiree slightly peeked one eye open and quickly realized she was literally on fire. Panic-stricken, she pulled away from the Northern Wind. "What have I done? How do I stop it?"

Desiree had never tried to calm her flames, nor had she ever blazed unknowingly. Seconds felt like hours and after many failed attempts to stop the fire, the Northern Wind shapeshifted back into wind form and tried to blow out her flames, but it only caused a firestorm.

Cries and screams for help became louder as her fire began to flick at the riders.

The thought of Desiree's fire hurting a human was unbearable to her, so without thinking, she stood on her seat and roared. "Stop!"

Her flames extinguished immediately. She slumped over with relief and looked around to see if anyone was injured. Every human remained unharmed but shaken with fear as the ride conductor rushed to bring everyone back to the platform.

Desiree anxiously jumped off the platform. *How can I let my fire get out of control? How can I cause such danger?* These thoughts raced through her mind. Then, flashing fire trucks boiling over with sirens surged onto the fair fields. She looked to the sky to find the Northern Wind, but the amusement rides swinging like pendulums cut her view. Fairgoers swarmed around her in disarray, rushing to exit.

Just as Desiree was about to faint from the dizzying madness, the Northern Wind suddenly grabbed her. "Come on, let's get out of here!"

"I can't breathe," Desiree said, pulling him back. "I'm still hot."

Realizing Desiree looked red as hot pepper, the Northern Wind urged. "Wait here, let me get you some water. Don't move!"

Desiree slumped over the side of a food truck, trying to calm herself. When the Northern Wind walked over with five bottles of water and a good portion of fried Oreos, she looked at the battered balls and sneered at him, grabbing the water.

"Come on. I thought it would cheer you up. Everyone is fine, Desiree. Nobody got hurt." The Northern Wind was trying to make light of the situation.

Desiree guzzled the third bottle of water and, as soon as she could catch her breath, said, "I just didn't know how uncontrollable…" She looked around paranoidly and, in a low voice, said, "*it* could get. My purpose is to make dreams come true with *it*, not to do *this*!"

"You are too hard on yourself. The most important thing is that you did control *it*. I saw you. You looked like a reigning Goddess when you commanded *it* to stop." He then got close to her and said, "I was proud of you. Now, look over there." The Northern Wind pointed to the *Tornado Twister*. "The ride is in mint tip-top of Texas shape. No one is hurt. The crew investigating the matter are scratching their heads — they don't know if what they witnessed was a mirage because everything is fine and well."

Desiree continued to drink water, unresponsive to what the Northern Wind said, remaining troubled in thought.

The Northern Wind hugged her and said, "Besides, we are still learning how to handle our special gifts, and these sorts of things happen to better our skills."

Feeling calmer, she looked up at the Northern Wind and devilishly teased, "Like you learning to better your landing skills?"

"There you are! My spitfire, she's back!"

Desiree, entirely calm, smiled with ease again. "Did I really look like a true Goddess? Striking my power?"

The Northern Wind laughed. "I wouldn't say you were striking… you were pretty shaky."

"You dirty gust!" She laughed, about to throw him a fireball, but looked around and decided to pinch him instead. Then she gave him a peck on the lips to distract him enough to snatch the basket of fried Oreos from his hand.

"Thief!" He exclaimed.

She giggled, put her arms around him, and with sincerity, said. "Thank you. Even though you don't ever really say much, when you do, it's always the right thing." Then she fed him a fried battered ball that oozed with melting Oreo cream.

"My! Almost as good as Claude's gooey treats." Popping one in her mouth.

"Do you feel better now?" Asked the Northern Wind as he wiped fried crumbs from his chin.

"Much," she said as she hugged him tightly. Then looked up at him, "What a pair we are. You with your crash landings and me with my wildfires. We are a natural disaster, you and I."

"Yes, but together we are a disaster in love." Said the Northern Wind.

Both were surprised to hear *Love* spill out of his lips. But despite the events, they kept on hugging each other.

"Come on, let's get out of here before they kick us out."

In better spirits, they raced each other to the exit, but just as they passed a dance hall, they heard their song playing loudly. Surprised, they peered in, and at the center of the dance floor, Maestro stood waving his hands.

"That wacky gadget! What's he doing here?" Said the Northern Wind.

"Maestro! We forgot about Maestro! I have to press *Stop*. He is still recording." She grabbed the Northern Wind's hand and led him to the center of the dance floor.

She then wrapped her arms over his shoulders, and he wrapped his arms around her waist.

Disco lights bobbled around them while their song bound their embrace.

Desiree gazed into the Greatest Wind's piercing blue eyes, playfully tossed his hair, and said, "You have thirty seconds before the song ends. Is there anything you would like to add to the mix?"

"I think we've added enough to the mix. I just want to keep holding you." The Northern Wind squeezed her tightly.

Then as the song nearly ended, she whispered in the Northern Wind's ear, "I love you too. Now and always. I love you."

Warped In Time

"Now and always. I love you." These words rang in the Greatest Wind's ear as Maestro's needle skipped in static, scratching the edges of the vinyl in time. The wheel spun again — clockwise — to fast forward. Maestro swung his arms, conducting and warping time to the present. The Greatest Wind's billows tumbled into an accelerated cycle of high speed.

Then all abruptly stopped. The Greatest Wind jerked as he opened his eyes. It took him a minute to sense he was no longer with Desiree, no longer at the State Fair and no longer in his past, but standing at the entrance steps of the Goddess of Desire's palace.

Violet and the Low Winds

Like a vapor, faintly seen, Violet observed the daily happenings of the Mystical Realm and reported them to her lady. Violet, a loyal lady in waiting, held the portal key to enter the Goddess's court. She was the gatekeeper, and any Low Wind sent from Night's court to gather a whisper from the Goddess had to go through her.

Violet was sipping her favorite humectant tea at the Belly's *Tea-N-Sip*, refueling her steam, when she overheard two Low Winds whistling with Gossip.

"I heard the Greatest Wind was spotted earthbound and is roaming over Texas." Said one of the Low Winds to the other while stirring its tea.

"Is that so… I wouldn't mind seeing those bad blue eyes roaming over me, honey!"

Their giggles rolled into laughter.

Violet suddenly made herself visible, smoking in her pink fume. "Excuse me, did you just say the Greatest Wind is earthbound?"

Startled to see Violet emerge from thin air, one of the winds spilled its tea. "Oh my! Hello there, Miss Violet; we didn't see you misting about. What brings you to the Belly of New York?"

"It's none of your concern what brings me here. But as you know, I have to report any matters of the mystical realm to the Goddess. So again, I ask, what is this I hear of the Greatest Wind being earthbound?"

"It has to be pure Gossip, Miss Violet, but yes, I heard from the Gust of the South that the Greatest Wind has left a Texas town in a wreckage."

The other Low Wind chimed in, "It has to be Gossip! The Greatest Wind hasn't made an earthbound appearance in over a decade. It's as if he forgot where he came from when he entered Night's court."

One Low Wind shushed the other. "Watch your breath! He is our commander, and we should respect that." Then turned to Violet, "Sorry, Miss Violet, we should be on our way."

"It's all right to speak frankly with me. Please don't leave. Sorry to be so short with you earlier. I suppose it's alright to tell you since we will make a formal announcement soon. But, we have just relocated the Goddess's portal here in the Belly of New York, and making new friends, especially charming Low Winds as yourself, is a great way to settle into this newness."

"The Goddess of Desire is here — in the Belly of New York? Oh, Miss Violet, we would love some whisper work, and it would be an honor to work with the Goddess. Please take our card." The Low Wind handed Violet her business card.

TWO LOW WINDS AND A GUST MOVING CO.
Movers. Shakers. Relocators
Please scan the barcode for more info.

"We are movers and transport and relocate furnishings when mystics travel earthbound, but whisper work would be a dream job. So please keep us in mind."

Violet had never met such hustling winds. It was refreshing to pick up on the energy of the Belly streets. "My! That's quite a business and one that is needed. How wonderful to see this type of entrepreneurial spirit here."

"We see it as a way to keep moving. What else to do while waiting for the Greatest Wind to send his orders? Toss takeout *Thank You* bags around?" Said the Low Wind.

A Gust in a van flew in front of the tea shop and honked as it parked, calling the Low Winds, "Come on! We're gonna be late!"

Both Low Winds rose from their seats. "That's our third. It was a pleasure chatting with you, Miss Violet, but we have to go. We have some magical tapestries to transport. Hopefully, we will be hearing from you soon."

"Yes, of course, and good luck with the move!"

Violet headed fast towards the Goddess's portal with the news of the Greatest Wind. But just as she was near the portal entrance, a bow shop full of silks, fringes, and ties lured her sights. Various scarves hung and were perfectly displayed and suited for an esteemed neck such as hers. *Maybe I'll just make a quick stop.* She thought to herself.

Later, Violet smoked through the Goddess's palace as a silk paisley scarf wafted behind her. "Goddess, my lady! I have the strangest news to tell you."

"Calm down, Violet. You're getting the palace humid and damp," the Goddess said as she took a double glance. "Is that a new scarf?"

"Yes, I'm sorry, my lady, I tried to rush to give you the news the fastest I could, but I guess I got tied up."

"Yes, I can see that." She changed the topic. "So what news are you smoking to tell me? Let me guess, is it that the Greatest Wind is on his way?"

Violet's scarf dropped to the floor. "What? The Greatest Wind is coming here?"

"Oh, wasn't that the news you were so steaming to report?"

Feeling guilty that she didn't know where this news came from, Violet couldn't help but fib as she stammered. "Of … of … of course, it is, my lady."

"It's truly fine, Violet. No need to work your new scarf into knots, but tell me, do you know what brings him this way?" The Goddess inquired very nonchalantly.

"Well … Umm … The Low Winds didn't have a clue. They overheard it through the Gust of the South that spotted the Greatest Wind in Texas."

Triggered by the mere mention of the lone star state, flames came soaring out of the Goddess's eye sockets. "Texas!"

"I should try to seek him out, my lady, and investigate the matter further. Besides, he can't enter your portal without me, and we haven't made a formal announcement of your new residency. There's no way he can track you." Violet headed to the door and grabbed the portal key.

"Hold on, Violet. There is no need for that. Let's not think much of it, but the Greatest Wind has access to my portal. No need to concern yourself. I just need you here to prepare for his arrival." The Goddess tried to keep calm, but the more she thought about the Greatest Wind in Texas, the more she became triggered.

Violet was shocked to hear the Greatest Wind had access to the Goddess's portal but decided not to pry. She could sense the distress in her lady's eyes and decided to turn matters into business. "How should I prepare for his arrival, my lady?"

The Goddess began to pace, deep in thought; *The tavern… Maestro… the song! Why now?*

Trying to get the Goddess's attention, Violet exclaimed, "My lady!"

Snapping out of it. "Oh, yes, Let's start by formally announcing my new residency to Night's court."

Violet took out her clipboard and began to take notes. Then noticing that the Goddess remained stuck in thought, she asked, "My lady, are you okay? I can turn him away if he makes you so uncomfortable."

The Goddess stopped pacing. "It's fine, Violet. I'm sure there is a good reason for this."

"Then how should I prepare the court for his arrival?" Violet repeated.

"Let's greet him like any high-ranking guest. Let's invite some mystics and give him a show!"

"Yes, let's, my lady!" said Violet as she became excited to make the palace come to life.

The Goddess's mind raced, wondering what Night was up to by sending the Greatest Wind to her. *It can't be whispering business.* But her only communication with Night's court was in matters of her whispers and even then, whispers were gathered by the Low Winds. *What could be so crucial in making the Greatest Wind return to Texas and relive the past? — our past.*

The Reunion

The Greatest Wind stood in front of the palace steps trying to recover from the fogginess of time travel. Desiree's embrace was still fresh in his memory, but he kept reminding himself that duty was the sole reason he was there. With each slow step he took towards the entrance of the Goddess of Desire's court, he could feel her flames brushing closer.

The whooping sound of brassy horns and jazz greeted him as he entered her palace. Fire-flappers fanned in dance while games of trickery and chance were played at various roulette tables. The Greatest Wind had never witnessed such a display of vanity, especially from a Goddess that wanted to live a simple life — this was quite the contrast.

The Goddess of Desire sat on her throne gilded in gold with a fiery garland flickering around her neck. She was no longer the vision of a young spitfire whom the Greatest Wind had known. Yet, underneath the polished surface, her nerves were getting the best of her.

Violet stood by the Goddess's side like a shield, waiting for the Greatest Wind to appear. "My lady, are you sure you're alright seeing the Greatest Wind again? I can still turn him away, or we can make him wait as long as you want."

"Thank you, my dear Violet, for your concern, but I'm quite alright. Besides, he is already here. We can't turn him away now. I can feel his cold chill in the air."

The Greatest Wind stood near, in the center court, watching her through the flames of the fire flappers in dance. He took notice of her beauty radiating through her court, and as captivating as she had become — he did not recognize the Goddess sitting on the throne.

Violet spotted him in the crowd and signaled for the music to stop. Guests of the court parted when they realized their honorary guest was in attendance.

Violet addressed The Greatest Wind. "We've been waiting for your arrival, Greatest, sir, as we heard you were visiting us. But just to let you know, it is standard protocol to enter this court through me. So what business do you have with the Goddess Desire this evening?"

The Greatest Wind became uncomfortable. He didn't realize the news of his arrival had leaked. "I am here, by order of Night, and I wish to conduct my business with the Goddess Desire in privacy."

Being suspicious of the Greatest Wind's request, Violet continued to address him. "Not following any protocol whatsoever and intruding upon the Goddess's portal raises my concern for the Goddess and her safety. Therefore, I see it best if you state your business now."

The Greatest Wind stood silent as he caught the gaze of the Goddess's amber-lit eyes that called to him as they once did, and for a brief moment, he saw his Desiree, which brought him comfort.

Violet impatiently repeated, "Sir, I will ask you again. What's your business with the Goddess of Desire?"

But the Greatest Wind had enough of the inquisition, and he had enough of all the fancies and grandeur on display. It was quite the juxtaposition from having just been time-warped from a rural Texas town to her palace with objects of desire at every corner. Without keeping his composure, he yelled, "Desiree! Enough!"

Gossip spread in waves throughout the court, "What did he just call her? Oh my! What private business must he want to conduct with the Goddess?"

Appalled by the Greatest Wind's lack of etiquette, Violet vaped in her words and stood with her jaw dropped to the floor.

The Goddess of Desire rose from her throne, striking her flames with dry directness, "Let us not forget, who you stand in front of, and whose court you stand foot on. State your business or leave my court at once!"

The Greatest Wind calmed his billows and bowed to her. "Forgive me for my tone, Goddess, it has been quite the journey to get to you, and it is with great importance and urgency that I see you at once in privacy as ordered by Night."

Intrigued by his request, the Goddess of Desire quickly turned to the court. "Thank you, everyone, for joining me in the evening festivities. It is now the hour of retirement."

The court disassembled, and all that glittered vacated the palace.

Violet continued to guard and stand by her lady.

The Goddess turned to Violet. "My dear Violet, you are dismissed as well."

"Are you sure, your grace?" asked Violet with concern.

The Goddess nodded with reassurance.

In a sarcastic tone, the Greatest Wind said, "Goodbye, Violet!" He then turned to the Goddess and gently smiled, "I can assure you the Goddess is safe with me."

Violet fumed, passing the Greatest Wind, hissing under her breath. "Blowhole!"

The Goddess Desire and the Greatest Wind finally stood alone and distantly faced each other. Both stoic in their stance reflected fire and ice in their glance.

"Well, you have my undivided attention. What is of dire urgency?" The Goddess of Desire tried to be firm in her words.

"It has been a long time. May I come closer?"

"Yes, you may approach," said the Goddess. Her pulse raced.

With each step, his temperature rose, causing his winds to set her fire ablaze. Then, uncontrollably, they began to tailspin into one another.

The Goddess quickly gathered her strength and transported them into her draftless salon, where Low Winds gathered whispers from her. The draftless room suppressed his strong winds and extinguished her flames, causing both to drop like flies.

Rumpled and disheveled, they landed flat on her rug and began to laugh at one another just as they once did.

"I forgot what happens when we get so close," said the Greatest Wind, chuckling.

"Yes, quite the collision," she said as she dusted herself and tried to regain her Goddess-like appearance. She pointed to the salon seating area and said, "This might be more fitting for our meeting. Please sit while I get us some refreshments."

"Yes, this much better," sarcastically remarked the Greatest Wind as he found himself uncomfortably billowing out of the arms of a small salon chair.

The Goddess found his foolishness comforting. "That's my chair. Winds sit over there," she said as she pointed to a larger and rounder lounge chair.

"Ah! Of course." He struggled to get up.

The Goddess poured tea for both of them. "I see you found Maestro? How is my music box?"

"Wacky as ever. I'm surprised you distanced yourself from that gadget. It was your favorite thing you possessed, but I suppose your taste has changed to the finer things." He teasingly said, looking around the room.

"Do you not find beauty in my palace?" asked the Goddess.

"I find it such a vanity for someone who once wanted to live a simple life."

The Goddess became insulted and sassed, "Yes, and I suppose your title had changed from when I knew you. Do you find vanity in such a title?"

The Greatest Wind nervously wheezed, realizing he had brought about a battle of the wits. So, to avoid any heat, he stayed quiet and drank his tea.

"Now, the reason you are here? Besides the obvious," the Goddess said as she sipped her tea.

"Obvious?" the Greatest Wind asked.

"Well … Duty," the Goddess said mockingly, still housing some bitterness from their sordid past. She tried to brush it off and said, "It would be funny if you were here to gather a whisper." She laughed.

He swallowed his tea in embarrassment and said, "Right … Well, your assumption is correct. I am here to gather a whisper."

The Goddess continued to laugh, thinking he was joking.

"What makes this so funny? This whisper is for Night's chosen one," he flatly said.

The Goddess nearly spit out her tea. "The chosen one?"

The Goddess was the only one that knew of the implication of such a whisper. Not even the Greatest Wind knew of the impact and importance of it, and she wondered what would make Night call for such an order. Then with concern, she asked, "How has Night been?"

"He has been ill and to be honest; I'm worried about his judgment. But then again, who am I to question Night?"

The Goddess became alarmed at the news. "Oh my! Has he been ill? That is very unlike Night. And what exactly about his judgment do you find so off?"

The Greatest Wind didn't know if he could speak as candidly as he once did with the Goddess but decided to take a chance, "I must alert you about his chosen one. I don't think he made the right choice."

She moved in closer to him and said, "Show me."

The Greatest Wind handed over his magical telescope and its receptors sucked her view into focus. Then the vessel glided, opening its crystal eye in search of Night's chosen one. First, it scanned the New York streets, following the trail of trampled candy wrappers and withered Cheeto crumbs. Then it slithered down the foulest corridors of an underground station, squeezing its scope through the grease-covered cracks of the metro train tracks until Night's chosen one came into view.

The Goddess pulled away from the magical telescope and gasped. "Is Night mad? This creature is — his chosen one?"

"I question that myself, but it is the reason why none of the heavens must know of this."

The Goddess Desire sat back and became stumped in thought. *What a twist of fate.* She had studied the complexity of people on Earth and had perfected her craft of whispers specifically for a human soul. Now, she would have to conjure her most critical whisper for the unthinkable — a creature of Night.

She turned to the Greatest Wind. "Please make yourself comfortable. It will take me some time to create a special whisper for our unique subject. But before I do that, I'm just going to take a quick minute to prepare myself." In suppressing her meltdown, she opened her portal window to the New York Belly streets, and with anguish and frustration, she let out a squawking yell. Then she simply shut the portal, composed herself and walked over to her tea cupboard.

The Greatest Wind found the act entertaining as it seemed her old self had returned, which made him more at ease.

The Goddess of Desire began experimenting and muddling various spices into whisper teas, but it all felt wrong for Night's chosen one. Frustrated, she opened her cupboard and blankly stared at all her loose teas, tinctures, and tonics, hoping the perfect tea blend would come to mind for such a creature.

A tin can in the back of the cabinet began to rattle to get her attention. She picked it up and pried the lid open. *Ah, yes! My earth root!*

She had forgotten about the root and had held onto it for sentimental reasons, but never found a reason to use it for any particular human whisper. *It's perfect for Night's chosen one!*

Immediately she began to grate it into a pile. Then, unexpectedly, the macaron spell of Nostalgia came rushing back and dragged her memory to the day she pulled the root from the earth's core — her Coronation day.

The Coronation

The Texas skies grew tiresome and gray while Desiree found herself waiting for the Northern Wind's return. Days felt like months, and weeks felt like an eternity, and still, the Greatest Wind hadn't returned from delivering a whisper. She was ready to go with him, but the summer heat set a blaze to her fire and to avoid any disasters decided to stay behind.

In a dream, the Moon Mother sang to her, letting her know she was with child. The following day, Desiree woke to find her belly in bloom. She joyfully sparked, knowing she would possess a title more significant than a Goddess; she would soon become a mother. She wanted to venture to seek The Northern Wind to let him know, but the travel was too much for her in her fragile state. To help, the Moon Mother sent Violet, from Moon's crater, as a gift to assist in the birth of the new heir. Both became excited to prepare for the child's arrival and wondered what type of God or Goddess the baby would become.

While Desiree slept, she had divine dreams of her child at play. One dream, they both frolicked in Moon's garden and brewed whisper tea together. They sat in miniature chairs made of calla lilies, when Desiree asked, "What should I name you, my dear child?"

Her child answered, "I am Destiny, Mama."

Desiree awoke with a smile, excited that Destiny, her child, would soon be in her arms.

But as she got close to her arrival date, Desiree broke with a fever hotter than her flames and became ill and weak. Violet tried to calm the fever by fanning her with the healing flower of echinacea.

Desiree, catching the breeze of the fanning echinacea flower, managed to blow a faint whisper, hoping the draft would send it drifting to the Northern Wind. "Come back to me. Come back for your family." She repeatedly whispered until the whisper began to drift.

As faint as the whisper was, it was determined to reach the Northern Wind's ear, even as it floated like a balloon, without the assistance and direction of any particular Low Wind; it drifted knowing that it would make its way in Divine Time.

On a beautiful pink moonrise, Desiree became in labor, ready to give birth to her child with Violet at her side. Pain struck her belly like lightning and as much as it hurt, she smiled, "Oh Destiny, you carry your father's strength," she said, rubbing her belly. But the pain continued to worsen, throbbing like something unnatural. She remained positive and tried to perk up for Destiny's arrival, but the pain became unbearable.

Violet urged and pleaded. "Please, my lady, keep pushing through this; little Destiny is almost with us."

With the vision of the Northern Wind holding Destiny in his arms, she gathered enough strength to press through the excruciating agony and with all her might, she pushed until Destiny was born. Then, she fell back in exhaustion and fainted as the pain settled.

When she woke, all was silent. "How's my baby, Violet? Why doesn't she cry out to the heavens? Please bring her to me."

With sorrow in her voice, Violet laid the baby in Desiree's arms. "My lady, I'm greatly sorry; the baby has not yet woken."

Tears of fiery wax streamed down the young Goddess's face as she saw her child for the first time and felt a love she had never experienced. "Please wake up, Destiny, my sweet child. Please wake up!"

Destiny laid silent and still and never woke to the earth. Desiree being in such an emotional state, rose with Destiny nestled in her embrace. Then, with the Moon's soft light leading the way, she walked the Earth forlornly.

The Moon Mother cried tears of milk as she didn't predict such a tragedy to occur to a young goddess-to-be.

When Destiny's body became cold, the Goddess entered Moon's garden, where miles of flowerscapes bowed to the young Goddess. They couldn't help but wilt in sadness as she passed through the garden, but in the far distance, tiger lilies sprung with life and that is where Desiree decided to say goodbye to her child. "I will be with you always," she whispered, laying Destiny on a bed of lilies that blanketed her.

In her heartache, she walked away from the lively greenery and headed towards the dry weeds that roamed like serpents. Standing on the dry, brittle dirt, she surrendered to her pain. She closed her eyes and purged her thoughts while the weeds slithered around her. Sadness wrapped tightly around her; then Anger pricked at her feet until its thorns covered her. With fiery tears streaming down her face, she thought of the Northern Wind one last time. Then the weed of Unforgiveness struck her limbs and pulled her under the biting soil, dragging her to the earth's boiling core.

Desiree's coronation into the Mystical Realm was set to arrive with the Blood Moon. The Moon Mother, not wanting her to miss it, had been showering and tending to the dry soil every moonrise while Violet assisted and misted it with her tincture.

When the time came, hours before the Blood Moon, Imperial roses emerged from the dead biting soil. The Moon, noticing the bed of deep red roses stretched for miles, became hopeful as her efforts in her late-night gardening paid off. *If the Goddess emerges now, she can still make it to the Night's court just in time for her coronation.*

To the Moon's surprise, a heavy rain showered over the garden, causing raindrops as large as marbles to hit the dry, cracked dirt — drumming the dead soil away in a hypnotic rhythm. The flowers swayed in tantric dance — swinging their leaves back and forth — calling to the great mystics for ceremonial rebirth — a call to Mother Earth.

The Earth's core rumbled in a pulse that got stronger and louder while flames ruptured from the Earth's surface. Then from the emerging fire, rose the Goddess of Desire, glistening like rubies as her flames arched like wings. She was no longer the young spitfire, no longer Desiree. She was the Goddess of Desire in true form.

The Moon Mother became moved when she saw her own Mother Earth greeting the Goddess of Desire, placing the earthly crown over the Goddess's head.

"The Earth clothes you with the crown of righteousness and the garment of fire. Today you become the Goddess of Desire. Do you pledge yourself to Mother Earth?"

She bowed her head. "Yes, I, The Goddess of Desire, vow myself to Mother Earth and to my crown."

The Goddess of Desire joyously smiled, renewed and anointed by the gracious Mother of all mothers. The Earth rejoiced as swarms of fireflies flew over the garden.

Violet, overcome with joyous tears, curtsied and said, "Your grace, welcome back."

"My dear Violet, thank you for being a loyal friend and not leaving my side."

Violet, so moved by her lady's comeback, couldn't say a word.

Then Orchids lifted the Goddess of Desire onto a petal chariot in celebration. Mother Nature joined the festivities and toasted to the Goddess anointed by Mother Earth, not by the Mystical Realm.

The Goddess renewed her appreciation of the living world and knew the serpent weeds would no longer bind her. She looked down at the tiger lilies and heard her daughter's cheerful voice say, "Congratulations, Mama!"

The Goddess of Desire responded in thought, "I will always carry you, my dear sweet girl."

Then she noticed a root dangling from her wrist. She plucked it and held on to it, knowing that more than her crown, it symbolized her coronation — her true rebirth to Earth.

The Whisper Seed

The Goddess of Desire's teapot came to a bellowing boil, snapping her out of the state of Nostalgia that continued to linger. She scooped the grains of the grated root and placed them into a sachet, which she dipped into her teacup of firewater. While waiting for the root tea to steep, she turned to the Greatest Wind and found him smugly sitting, which irritated her in thinking of their sordid past. She still didn't know why he never returned to her that fateful summer. Scorching in the thought, phantom serpent weeds pricked at her feet about to drag her under again. Then Moon's advice rang in her ear: *Move forward with love. The only way you can dissolve this is with Love.*

The Greatest Wind, noticing the Goddess conflicted in thought, asked, "Is everything alright with the whisper tea?"

She then debated if she should tell the Greatest Wind about Destiny, but decided it was best to keep matters strictly business, being that she knew the sole reason he was there was out of duty. So she changed her tone and tried to come from a place of Love. She exhaled and smiled. "Yes, everything is well and ready." Then walked toward him with the root tea. "You must stay seated and try not to wiggle, as it might prick and tickle."

"Yes, I remember what it's like to carry your whispers," he reminded her.

"Ah yes, but that was some time ago. This whisper is different, it's a whisper seed, and something this small to make is more potent to take. Must I remind you of the side effects?"

"As far as I can recall, it's like a truth serum?" He said this as he made himself more comfortable.

"Yes, that is one of the side effects. It also might activate your fury. Try to calm your winds." She said, worrying how the whisper seed would affect a strong wind like the Greatest.

"How long should the effects last?"

The Goddess propped herself on his lap. "No longer than an hour, and I would wait to deliver the whisper after that time."

Surprised by her boldness, he wheezed. It had been so long since she sat perched on his lap.

"Are you ready?" She asked with a gentle smile.

He took one last whiff of her rosy scent and one last glance of her amber eyes as he wasn't sure when he'd have the opportunity to be so close again. "Yes, ready."

She took a large sip of her root tea and swished it in her mouth until it spun into a whisper seed. Then she pressed her heart-shaped lips against his ear and began to whisper.

The Greatest Wind closed his eyes as he felt the tufts of the whisper hum in his ear. At first, it felt like silk tendrils gently tickling in its flow, but then it began to drill and throttle its way. The Greatest Wind found himself overcome by a strong urge to embrace the Goddess as he once did, to kiss the Goddess as he once did, but he fought the urge knowing it was the power of the whisper seed.

"It's almost over. Hold tight." She said to reassure him.

The experience of it all seemed just as he remembered it to be, loving and nurturing. Until — pain struck. So penetrating and sharp — pain filled every inch of his billows. He pried himself off the chair, pushing the Goddess off his lap. "You tricked me! What have you put in me?" The Greatest Wind rumbled.

"I told you, whisper seeds are not an easy pill to swallow. You must rest," warned the Goddess.

The Greatest Wind lost his temper as the whisper seed was causing unsettled feelings to fester. "You laced the whisper seed with Feelings! You witch! Heretic! What did you put in me?"

Even though the Goddess of Desire knew the effects of the whisper seed were making the Greatest Wind ill in his words, she wondered if the whisper seed had activated the truth.

After minutes of hearing the Greatest Wind huff, she couldn't bear it any longer. It hurt her deeply. "I'm quite tired and would like to rest. I suggest you do the same. You have the whisper seed now. You may go and deliver it."

Even though the draftless salon held back the Greatest Wind's force, his blows gathered speed.

The Goddess called for Violet, who quickly shot into the room, "Violet, please show our guest the way out."

"Certainly, your grace," she said as she bowed to her lady. Then scowled at the Greatest Wind, wanting to escort him right out of existence.

The Greatest Wind continued his rampage. "I'm not leaving until you tell me what you did to me! Is it not enough that I jumped through the hoops of time to find you! And endured that dreadful song! But now you have infected me with the most bitter poison — Feelings!"

"Sir," Violet said as she nudged him. "It's time for you to leave, and I think you should leave through the back door."

Violet tugged the loom rug under the Greatest Wind's billows, and a portal chute slid open. The Greatest Wind clasped himself to a chair, refusing to leave, but the earth's gravity sucked him right into the chute, causing him to fall aimlessly towards the Belly streets of New York.

"Desiree, Desiree! Are you a friend or foe?" The Greatest Wind repeatedly shouted as he spun out of control.

Violet peeked down the portal chute as the Greatest Wind continued to descend and sarcastically responded, "That would be *foe*, like *fo sho*! See ya, blowhole!" Then with concern turned to the Goddess. "How are you feeling, your grace?"

No longer feeling the effects of Nostalgia, and no longer feeling tied to her past, the Goddess of Desire's flames rose high. "I feel free." She replied.

The Greatest Wind descended rapidly, unable to control his winds. He targeted a large metal dumpster and threw lightning at it causing its rubbish to fly mid-air and break his fall. But still, he crashed right into the trash bin knocking himself unconscious, while the magical telescope plummeted onto the hard pavement — shattering.

When the pain of the whisper seed subsided, the horrendous scent of rotting filth woke the Greatest Wind. Sore, smelly, and warped with exhaustion — there was nothing more he wanted to do other than to deliver the whisper seed and return to Night's court. So he grabbed the telescope and looked down its crystal lens to locate Night's chosen one, but its eye remained shut. Then he noticed the shattered body parts. In a twisting fit of rage, he yelled to the heavens: "WHERE. IS. THAT. VERMIN!?!"

Destiny and the Greatest Wind

Weeks had passed, and the whisper seed had remained undelivered. The longer the Greatest Wind carried the whisper seed, strange events began to unfold. Birds flew alongside him rather than distance themselves from his cold chill. Stars shot straight through him, invigorating his strength. Rather than fear him, the Earth welcomed him with warmth and light.

At first, the Greatest Wind brooded as he liked to be feared. But little by little, as the whisper seed settled, his heart began to open up to its charm, and when it did, the most wondrous thing of all happened. While he slept, he began to dream of a little girl who skipped with her monarch butterflies and would come to play with him.

Sometimes they played card games, and as tiny and innocent as she looked, she liked to cheat when the Greatest Wind wasn't looking.

"I win. Again!" She would say.

"I give up, kid." So the Greatest Wind would say, stumped how she would win at every hand.

When the Greatest Wind took long-winded naps, the little girl liked to sneak into his dreams and play tricks on him. Sometimes she would decorate his billows with her butterflies or fluff and color them into shades of pastels. Unaware, he wondered why the Lands, Trees, and the Seas laughed at him with salutations. Until he would catch a glance of himself through a pond's reflection, then realize the trickster child got him again. He felt like a father to the little girl who came to him in his dreams, which helped ease his frustrations with the broken telescope. Without it, he had no way of locating Night's chosen one. He spent his days working hard to repair the telescope parts but failed at every attempt.

Until one day, the child marched into his dream dragging in a toolbox, and said with the brightest of smiles, "Your parts came in today. We shall fix your telescope."

She handed him a booklet of the oddest configurations titled, *How To Fix A Broken Magical Telescope*. Both worked together, tattering at the device, replacing every shattered part until it stood in perfect shape.

Finally fixed, the Greatest Wind gratefully said, "Child, thank you for your help. What is your name to call you by?"

The child picked up her toolbox and replied, "You are welcome, Greatest sir. My name is Destiny. You may call me by that name." Then she waved goodbye as her butterflies trailed behind.

It was such a vivid dream that the Greatest Wind awoke in giggles, which alarmed him, fearing the whisper seed was causing him to become giddy and delusional. Still, as he turned to his nightstand, he wheezed when he noticed the magical telescope was in mint condition.

He quickly grabbed it and looked down at its lens. At first, the body jerked, but then its crystal eye opened and with an oily rub the telescope began to roam freely.

"Alright, now, find me that creature of Night." He commanded. The telescope mapped Night's chosen one and revealed its location in no time.

The Open Fan

The wildflowers were in bloom, indicating that it was the courting season. All of the Goddesses of the Mystical realm were hosting evening parties looking for their suitors. The courting season was something the Goddess of Desire usually mocked and was grateful to be far removed from residing on Earth. So hesitantly, she asked Violet, "Are you sure about this?"

Violet saddled a Jetstar fueled with stardust and prepared for take-off. "Yes, my lady, it's time we find you a suitor and join the rest of the realm. Hosting an Open Fan Soiree is the perfect way to get you back into societal graces."

As reluctant as the Goddess of Desire was, she knew Violet was right. It was time to reconnect with Night's court and hosting a soiree would be the perfect way to do just that. Typically, the Goddess of Desire held private affairs and kept her portal locked, with Violet holding the portal key. But this evening would be different. The Goddess would open her gateway for any mystical soul to attend the soiree.

Violet strapped a helmet on and secured herself. "I'm ready, my lady. Light me up!"

"Hold on tight, Violet. This star is a wild one!" The Goddess of Desire lit the fuse, sending the Jetstar bucking straight into Night's sky.

When the Jetstar reached the corner of Night's blank canvas, Violet began to paint the Goddess of Desire's invitation. Etched in Violet's smoky pink hue that twinkled with stardust residue, the invitation read:

Tonight the Goddess Desire favors your presence
Open Fan Soiree
Bring your flirtiest flare!
Portal open to All

The Goddess of Desire stood in her garnet gown while Violet tugged at its corset straps, trying to lace her up.

"Do you think anyone will show?" The Goddess nervously imploded herself to fit into the dress.

"Night's court, reject a soiree? During courting season? Never." Violet tied the last lace on the Goddess's dress.

"But would they reject me? Why wouldn't they? After all, I haven't shown up to Night's court and turned down many invitations in the past. I wouldn't blame them for not showing up."

"Yes, your grace, but you forget you are a Goddess. That title is something sacred in the Mystical Realm. Everyone is curious about the Goddess who left Night's court and reigns with her fire. So why would they want to miss out on an opportunity to get to know you?"

"Violet, I don't know what I would do without you. You are truly my treasure." Said the Goddess of Desire, grateful to her lady in waiting for her encouraging words. Then the Goddess glanced in the mirror, "My! Quite the hotdog suit. This dress won't do."

"Your grace, we don't have much time. I have to open the portal gates." Violet said, beginning to stress.

"Don't worry about me, Violet. I think I'll just shapeshift into something fiery. I'll leave you to take care of the party duties."

"Yes, your grace, I'll let you get ready." Violet smoked over to the ballroom to make sure everything was in order.

The palace flourished with Victorian romance. Blushed roses entwined every column, ruby chandeliers hung like vines, and candles lit like starbursts reflected onto the mirrored walls and marble floors that were chalked for an evening of dancing.

"It's perfect!" Said Violet to the court staff, shuffling to get the palace ready.

Then, Violet turned to the royal symphony, plucking at their instruments. "Is everyone ready to play magically tonight?"

The composer passionately replied, "Yes, miss Violet. The string section will pull, rip and tear out their hearts! Until everyone finds love."

"That's a bit dramatic, but I'll leave you to it. I'm off to turn the key!" Violet excitedly made her way to the portal gate. When she got to the gateway, she checked to see if the coast was clear. Then, with no one watching, she molded herself to fit the portal lock — with a wiggle, turn and snap, the lock unhinged itself.

The gateway slid open, and a grand parade of victorious chariots entered the palace grounds. It was a high-profile lineup that included the Ladies, Lords, Gods, and Goddesses of Night's court as well as celebrity appearances from the Constellation Stars.

Violet announced every guest as they entered the palace.

First, the Ladies of the Night emerged from their jetstar chariot carrying their fans in various fashions, some with the flirtiest plumes and others with folding silks in ornate constellation patterns and shapes. Next, the Lunar Goddesses entered the palace twirling their fans of effervescent moonlight diamonds, while the Constellation Stars brightened the court, fanning their specular light. Every Lady and Goddess was in attendance, including Morning Star, the Goddess formerly known as Venus.

Then the Gods and Lords of Night entered with their mighty swords in one hand and millinery hats in the other. The God of Dusk tipped his smoking topper as Violet announced him. While the North Star carried his five-pointed opera hat and headed towards the food trays. The well-known brother duo, The Big Dipper and Little Dipper, made a grand arrival, dipping their empire hats at every Lady and Goddess they passed.

"Pardon me, pardon me, coming through with hot macarons," said Claude as he replenished the glass display of aphrodisiac macarons.

Hands from every angle grabbed at the sweets as fast as they could, being it had been some time they had Claude's spellbound macarons.

"Claude, we must find a way to get you back into court. You don't deserve to be cast out. Besides, no pastry chef can craft a macaron like you." So said the God of Dusk just as he bit into a *Charred Rose* macaron that woke his seven senses. "My God, you truly have a gift."

Claude graciously smiled, continuing to replenish the trays while the Lords and Ladies of Night levitated around the table, ingesting Claude's *Fluffy Cloud* macarons.

Then fire sirens rang, indicating the Goddess of Desire was entering her court. The silence broke as she gracefully stepped into the ballroom, fanning her steel-pointed brisé fan, lit at every point like torches. All bowed to the Goddess of Desire as they marveled at her radiant fire.

She sat perfectly composed on her throne, with flames rising like a phoenix. Then she scanned the palace, pleasantly surprised at everyone in attendance. All flittering in their exotic flair, they waited for the Goddess of Desire to commensurate the game of courtship.

Claude bowed to the Goddess and presented her with a *Fire Arrow* macaron crafted just for her. "My lady, a macaron to ignite the flames?"

The Goddess cautiously examined it and asked, "Is there any Nostalgia in this?"

Claude grinned and replied, "No, your grace. It's made with your own fiery spices, specially crafted for you."

The Goddess took a small bite and felt her flames burst into Cupid's bow and arrow. "Lovely Claude, this is exquisite. Thank you." She flooded with relief as the spell was harmless.

Then the Goddess of Desire addressed the court without words but with a mere gesture. She slid off her scarlet glove, laid her closed fist to rest on its wrist, and slowly uncurled her fingers to reveal her open palm. It was a symbolic gesture of one's readiness to find their match and the perfect way to commensurate such an evening — the open hand. Applause and shouts of *Bravo!* Echoed throughout the palace for the Goddess of Desire's return to society. And with her open hand and a fluttering fan, the game of courtship began.

A closed fan and an eye roll meant a Goddess was not interested. The half-open fan suggested potential, but a wide-open fluttering fan said love was in the works. It was all one needed to know to play the game, but the subtleties of the flutter mixed with the expression made it an art form.

From the signals and cues of the fan, the Gods and Lords of Night's court engaged with their language of millinery gestures. The flirtation began with a bow and hat in hand. A tilting of the back of the hat meant farewell, but a hat held at heart indicated a surrender to love.

Fanology was one of the few subjects the Goddess of Desire excelled at in prep school, and as much of a master of the subject as she was, she kept her fan wide open. She didn't have the heart to close her fan, so she kept it open and listened to each God and Lord that dared to fan her flame. Soon enough, she found herself delightfully fitting into the realm. Mingling with the rest wasn't as bad as she thought. So with cheer and laughter buzzing around her court, she found herself dancing the evening away.

But then, Gossip fluttered her fan with a poisonous utterance. "Her flames are untamable. She's a vagabond. How will she ever find her match? The Greatest Wind even found her grace to be nothing more than wildfire."

It was a sting that cast a shadow on her mood, and the Goddess Desire excused herself and went out to the balcony to catch the cityscape of the New York Belly. She loved accessing the human world when she wanted to escape and shapeshift into someone other than a Goddess. She fantasized about who she would shapeshift into next. Would it be a dressmaker, Wall Street trader, or maybe even Claude's next sous chef? She giggled at the thought.

She then looked to Night's sky, wondering if she would ever fit into the realm and find love again. She closed her eyes to make a wish, which was not the sort of thing a Goddess would do. It was quite a foolish act in the Mystical Realm, but the Goddess was not above anything foolish.

So just as she was about to make her wish, a strong wind caught her fiery fan and sent it flying in mid-air, causing its flames to blow out. She was overcome with joy as it felt like something the Greatest Wind would pull off. But to her surprise, when she opened her eyes to greet the Greatest Wind, she was met with a tall night in a coattail suit of the darkest black.

"Goddess of Desire, you look radiant tonight," said the Darkest Night as he bowed, holding his classic top hat at his heart.

Even without her fan, the Goddess fluttered at the handsome sight of the Darkest Night.

"Am I late?" he asked with a dimpled smirk.

The Goddess's brightest flames could not hide her cheeks that blushed. "Hi, hello, late?" She quickly regained her composure and said, "What is late to the Divine hour of the clock?"

The Darkest Night began to laugh. "Agreed," he said.

"Thank you for attending my party, your majesty. I've heard about you. It's funny how we have never met." The Goddess curtsied.

"You don't need to curtsy, that sort of greeting is for my brother, Night. We might have never met, but I've seen you. I've watched you. You have captivated me for some time," said the Darkest Night so boldly.

The Goddess of Desire deflected as her cheeks flamed in crimson. "Oh, I'm sorry, I'm sure I would have seen you. Where exactly did you see me?"

"Well, I did keep hidden, always kept hidden. But I've been there, even during your darkest hour."

The Goddess turned, glancing down the balcony towards the tiger lilies where Destiny lay in Moon's garden. She wondered if the Darkest Night truly knew of her darkest hour.

The Darkest Night walked behind her to console her. "Yes, I was there when you laid your child to rest and I made sure you would not miss your coronation for it. So I had the Mother of all earthly mothers anoint you."

The Goddess became touched by the Darkest Night's kindness. "That was by your hand? You did that? Thank you, Darkest Night, your majesty, but I must beg you not to tell anyone of that event in my life. It's already bad enough I am referred to as Fallen, simply by choosing to have my portal on Earth."

The Darkest Night looked deep into her amber-lit eyes. "And yet, that is what makes you glorious and perfect. I couldn't stay hidden any longer. I had to come to you while I had the chance, while your portal was open to all. I only hoped I wasn't too late."

The Goddess Desire melted hearing the Darkest Night's gentle words and replied with boldness. "It seems Divine Time is on our side."

He reached for her hand, kissed it and led the Goddess of Desire back into the ballroom, where they dazzled together in unity.

New love unfolded, and so did the fans that fluttered with the latest season of matches made. Even Claude floated with smoking romance as he escorted Violet to the ballroom floor.

In merriment, all danced the evening away.

The Lark and the Greatest Wind

Car alarms set off for miles when the Greatest Wind struck the city street.

"You have arrived at your destination." Announced the telescope.

He looked around to see where he was, but the thickness of the early morning fog didn't let his sights get too far. Nevertheless, he knew for sure he was in proximity to the Belly of New York, judging by the short distance of the trip and his inability to pick up speed without smashing into city traffic, newsstands, and skyscraping buildings.

"Turn onto Fourth Street. Go straight for three blocks. Turn Right. Turn Left. Turn Right. Turn Left," said the telescope on loop.

Like a pinball, he bounced and bumped into every light post, trying to follow directions. *Unfortunately, delivering a whisper isn't as easy as it used to be.* He realized his girth and strength would make it difficult to move through the tight streets without causing a ruckus. He thought about taking the risk and shapeshifting into a human or even a Low Wind to make it easier. But whispers had to be delivered while in his true form; otherwise, he could potentially lose it. Frustrated, he brooded and revved his winds.

"Hey! What's going on down there? Turn that motorcycle off! I'm calling the cops if you don't stop!" yelled a resident from a brownstone window.

"You tell 'em' Al! This is the West Village! Have some respect!" scolded another, as the window slammed shut.

The Greatest Wind remained still, trying not to make the slightest of puff. After all, the last thing he needed was human attention, and he certainly couldn't run the risk of scaring off Night's chosen one. So he sucked in his billows and moved as slowly as possible, trying to float and not collide into any trash bin, post, hydrant, or street trinket in his path. As much as it ruffled his billows to be so cautious, the upside was that he could sense Night's chosen one was near. The whisper seed had begun to waddle and shift, indicating it was getting ready for its delivery. So he turned off the telescope and let the whisper seed take the lead.

While carefully zig-zagging through the streets, he inspected every crevice and dark corner in search of the chosen one, but the whisper seed remained unresponsive.

A wilting light post flickered over a park gate and, in mystical Morse code, transmitted:

"... Enter... Enter... It lays here...."

He thanked the Light Post and swung open the screeching gate. The park hazed with an incandescence of smog and city greenery, while a labyrinth of park benches outlined its concrete path. The trees cackled as the Greatest Wind stepped foot into Washington Square Park. Then began the chorus of a Lark, singing off-key and ever so awkwardly. With the spotlight of the full moon and a bellflower that is used as a microphone, the Lark sang high on a tree and low in pitch.

Feelings, nothing more, nothing less than a Feeling?

What's it like? Greatest Wind, to have such a feeling?

We would like to know. Won't you tell us?

What's it like for a wind to have

Feelings — Feelings — Feelings

Awestruck by the odd lounge act of the Lark, the Greatest Wind decided to ignore it and look for Night's chosen one.

"Wrong move, buddy," said the Oak Tree as it blocked the Greatest Wind's path.

"Excuse me?" said the Greatest Wind, confused by the Oak Tree's aggressive temperament.

"The Lark has sung. We suggest you answer what it wants to know," barked the Oak Tree.

"I think I'll just mind my own business and search for what I need to find," firmly said the Greatest Wind as he took a peek under a park bench.

The Oak Tree snapped its limbs. "Wrong! One thing you need to know, Wind, this is a city park — Washington Square Park — manmade — and not under the jurisdiction of the Mystical Realm. We do things differently here. So have some respect."

"But I don't understand what the Lark wants to know. Winds do not carry feelings; we carry whispers and I am here to deliver one," said the Greatest Wind flatly.

The Lark nearly choked on his chorus, then began to laugh hysterically and spoke. "Do you mean to tell us that you are unaware you carry feelings?"

The Greatest Wind turned to address the Lark, and said, "I can assure you, I do not. But I am carrying a potent whisper, burning to be let out, so if you kindly can let me get to my business."

The Lark's crescent eye bulged with its seer. "Do you think I can't see? I can see clearly and right through your billows. You are lying to me and even worse to yourself. Tell me! What feeling do you possess?"

The whisper seed began to throttle and move up towards the Greatest Wind's throat, so he decided to be truthful to Lark to get back to his search quickly. "I suppose … I feel … anxious … Anxious, to deliver the whisper. I must do so promptly."

The Lark squawked. "If that is what troubles you, we have the receiver — the recipient of your whisper. If you want us to help you, I suggest you start to answer my questions better."

"Why do you want to know about feelings?" asked the Greatest Wind.

The Oak Tree snapped, "Have you lost your billows? Nobody questions the Lark."

"I didn't mean to disrespect the park nor the Lark. I am just trying to carry out my duty.

And for the sole purpose of duty and time, I will gladly answer your question. Lark, if you can kindly repeat the question once more," said the Greatest Wind, eager to get to Night's chosen one.

In a game show host manner, the Lark spoke. "You carry a feeling that none of us carry, nor any wind we have ever come across. What — is — that — feeling?"

The Greatest Wind's billows slumped to the ground with great shame as he stammered, "Lo… Love." Then he raised his head to the Lark to explain. "But it is more of a curse than a feeling."

The Lark jumped off the tree branch and circled the Greatest Wind to assess him. Then, in flight, he chirped. "There was a time you didn't see it as a curse. There was a time you carried Love with happiness. What happened for that to change?"

Puzzled by the riddling of the Lark, the Greatest Wind said, "I don't know what you mean. I answered your question. Please let me…."

The Lark interrupted as he landed on the Oak Tree's shoulder. "You don't need to explain. You just need to show me." Then, with its seer, he intensely inspected the Greatest Wind. "What's that shiny object dangling on your wisp?"

The Greatest Wind looked at his billowy finger. "It's my Code of Honor Ring that I received from Night's Army."

"Hand it over to me. Let me take a look at it," said the Lark as he signaled for the Oak Tree to grab it.

The Greatest Wind begged the Lark as he handed over the ring. "Please just let me deliver the whisper. Timing is of the essence."

The Lark ignored the Greatest Wind as its eye crystalized in the seer, examining every scratch and etch on the gold-casted ring. "I see. I see perfectly," said the Lark, as the Greatest Wind's Code of Honor ring began to tell the story.

The Tornado and the Northern Wind

Like a whizzing breeze, the young Northern Wind flew through an open window, funneled up a staircase, and drafted into a bedroom without a peep. There asleep laid his target — a keyholder — a human with a strong will. Desiree's words rang through him: *The ones that carry keys have the power to generate a domino effect of change.*

It pleased the Northern Wind to deliver whispers that would instill bravery in those that would change history for the greater good. So with a smirk of confidence, he aimed his billows and swiftly shot the whisper into the human ear. *Bullseye!* He took out his magical telescope and watched the whisper make its way through the human body and come alive.

Didn't even flinch, he just kept sleeping. The Northern Wind proudly reflected on his successful mission. He couldn't wait to return to Desiree and celebrate, so he flew fast, nonstop until he hit the Texas lands. There he made a pit stop at their favorite pond, where Desiree liked to collect flowers for her tea. While he refueled his winds and plucked daisies for Desiree, he caught his reflection from the stillness of the pond. He couldn't help but stare deeply at himself as his strength grew daily. While he inspected every billow and wisp, he discovered it — a lingering fuzz — it was the size of a walnut and pinkish in hue. *What the heck?*

Suddenly, the still water turned rapid as the grumble of the harshest winds came in from a distance. He greeted the unfamiliar winds with a nod as they stampeded past him. Then, the sky changed and fell gray, inverting itself into a funneling freight of a Texas Tornado.

"It's time. It's time for your draft," said the Tornado as it unrooted everything in its path.

The Northern Wind couldn't bear the thought of leaving Desiree without telling her that he loved her once more so he fought against the grasping clutches of the Tornado. He pushed and pushed and just as he could see Desiree's Tavern in the near distance, he was met with the harsh winds that charged toward him and dragged him into the tornado's massive vortex.

"No! Let me go! I just have to do one last thing," cried the Northern Wind.

The Tornado pulled him right to its eye, "Let me get a closer look at you, boy. I've heard all about your mighty strength," said the Tornado as he looked at the Northern Wind up and down. "You don't look so strong to me, boy. Does he, troops?"

In unison, the army troop of winds shouted: "No, sir."

"Why did you flee from me when I called you, boy?" the Tornado asked.

The Northern Wind hesitated to tell him about Desiree and found himself stammering.

"Answer me, boy!" said the Tornado, growing impatient.

"I just wanted to say goodbye… to a friend, sir."

The Tornado brought him closer and magnified its eye. "What's that I see in your billows, boy?" The Tornado examined his winds closely. "Why, that looks like a spark of some sort —Wait — Is that? Could that be? — Love?"

The troop of winds began to laugh and heckle the Northern Wind.

Embarrassed by the one person he was looking forward to impressing, the Northern Wind denied it. "No, sir, I can reassure you. I don't possess such a thing."

The Tornado continued to drill the Greatest Wind. "Boy, is this what you picked up this summer? By delivering whispers for the soon-to-be Goddess of Desire."

He was shocked that the Tornado knew of their union. "How… did you?"

"I know everything about my soldiers. Did you think you were a match for a Goddess, boy?" The Tornado chuckled. "All you would've been to her was a messenger — a servant. You should be kissing the trails of my wreckage that I scooped you in on time." The Tornado funneled around the Northern Wind. "Isn't that right, troops?"

"Yes, sir!" The troops shouted.

Defending his stance, the Northern Wind boldly said, "I found there is honor in such a service, sir. And I had the pleasure of delivering whispers to human souls that will one day change the world for the greater good, sir."

"Honor in such a service? This is the almighty Night's Army of Winds. Only the best of winds can be part of Night's Army. Whisper work is for Low Winds! But if you want to continue to be a messenger, it's your choice. So what's it gonna be? Do you want to be a whisper boy, servant to the Goddess of Desire? Or do you want to be a soldier of the Night's Army?"

The Northern Wind wanted nothing more than to see his Desiree one last time, but this was his path and he couldn't be seen as weak, not in the Army's eyes and especially not by Night. So as much as it saddened the Northern Wind not to say goodbye to his Desiree, he stepped in line with the rest of the army winds and stomped his billows as he declared, "I want to be a soldier of the Night's Army, sir!"

"Well, that's a better attitude! Whisper work and that awful love fuzz you're lugging around are behind you. So don't you worry, boy, soon enough, you'll be thanking me."

The Northern Wind stood stoic and, with a blank stare, winded off. "Yes, sir!"

In time, to prove himself to the Tornado and the Army, he became a cold front — denying any Feeling he possessed. Love became his worst opponent. He fought his Love and became fierce and relentless in force. He tore through cities, nations, and countries and even cut through the same Texas bridges he stood on with Desiree. He became wicked to the wisp and bad to the billow.

The Tornado boasted proudly of his prodigy and awarded the Northern Wind with the Code of Honor ring.

"You have proven yourself, boy. I reward you with this ring to remind you of just that. How far you have come. Aren't you relieved that you replaced that Love fuzz with this?"

"Yes, sir!" Piped the Northern Wind as he accepted the ring. But just as he put it on his billowy finger, Desiree quickly popped into his mind, which triggered Feelings. This upset him, so he made a pact that he would no longer think of her.

With a bitter and cold front, he flew so high, surpassed the stars, and stormed into Night's heavens causing it to rain. It had never rained in the heavens before that time, which made the act a miracle event. This got the attention of Night, that upon the Northern Wind's graduation from the Army, knighted him with the title – The Greatest Wind.

The Creature of Night

With a blink, the Lark's crystal eye returned to its regular crescent shape. The story behind the Code of Honor Ring saddened the Lark. "It's a shame, Wind. You don't see what I see, but in time you will." The Lark tossed the Greatest Wind's ring back to him with its beak. Then the Lark flew to a Birch tree and began to prepare its voice for a song.

The Greatest Wind didn't know what to make of the park Lark, but he did as the Lark asked, and now he needed to hold the Lark to its promise. "You said you would help me if I answered your questions. Will you now help me locate what I am here for?"

"Ah, yes! The matter of the recipient. I almost forgot the reason you think you are here and the purpose you think you are serving." Then the Lark signaled to the park with a bird call. "Can we show the Wind where the recipient is?"

Bellflowers elegantly rang from a garden patch and chimed, "It lays here."

Then the Lark requested, "Can we light his path? To make it easier for the Wind?"

The Light Post threw its dim spotlight over the bellflowers that rang louder to get the Greatest Wind's attention.

"You may now make your delivery," chirped the Lark.

Finally, he had clearance from the city park and even though the whisper began to burn, he was relieved that his journey would soon be over. The Greatest Wind slowly made his way, grazing through the grass, breezing past the trees while the whisper seed began to climb up his throat. Finally, the glowing bellflowers parted, uncovering Night's chosen one that lay unconscious on the soil. *There you are, in your vermin filth as I knew I would find you,* thought the Greatest Wind as he stared down, brooding with contempt. For Night's chosen one wasn't a human, wasn't even a keyholder. Night's chosen one was a city rat. And a bloody rat at that.

"What happened to it?" asked the Greatest Wind.

The Bellflowers chimed. "We don't know. We've tried to nurse it, but he looks in bad shape. Our guess is he got into some sort of fight."

The Greatest Wind poked the rat and it flinched, moaning in pain.

"Well, at least it's alive," said the Greatest Wind in disgust. He shook his head and rumbled in disbelief. *Out of all duties, I'm delivering a whisper to a Rat!* He then got close to the rat's fuzzy ear and just as he inhaled to shoot out the whisper seed, pollen got caught in his throat causing him to sneeze. The whisper seed flew out, birling into the park. "No!" he shouted. He followed it, floating, trying to grasp at it. But the whisper seed managed to escape the Greatest Wind's clutches. It bounced off a park bench, then got caught in the leaves of the Oak Tree. It nearly drifted out of the park when the Greatest Wind, in a panic, inhaled his wind so deeply he just about guzzled up the entire park. Grateful to catch the escape artist of the whisper seed and avoid another delay, he handled the whisper seed delivery with care.

He hovered over the rat and, in an apologetic tone, said, "I'm still unsure what to make of Night's decision, but I have to put my faith in him, and I now bow down to Night's chosen one. May you use this whisper seed wisely, Rat." Then the Greatest Wind aimed and swiftly shot the whisper seed straight into the rat's ear. "Bullseye!" The Greatest Wind exhaled with relief. "Finally, I'm free of this duty." He fled with fury, without a glance back at the park or the strange Lark, and headed towards the Night's sky.

The Divine Clock

Amid time and space, the Divine Clock peaked from all darkness with its quartz tower that rang like crystal tubular bells. It was Night's sacred place where he would join the Sun for an eclipse, one of the few times they could come together as one. Upon arriving, he would enjoy his night drive through the ethereal crystalline grounds, marveling at the cloisters of the timescape.

But on the top hour of a rare eclipse — the Black Moon eclipse — Night rushed to enter the Divine Clocktower rather than enjoy his drive. He hastily scaled the spiraling stairs, which were laden with bookshelves filled with histories. He usually liked to grab a book at random and reminisce while he waited for the Sun, but on this occasion, he searched for one book in particular. He rummaged through the shelves, desperately trying to remember where he hid it in centuries past. Then it came to him. "The Clock's hands! They point straight to it."

As he followed the hand of Time, it led him straight to the den mantel, "Yes, right where I hid it." Night remembered disguising it in a linen book cover titled *Book of Roses*. He pulled it off the shelf and dusted it off, unraveling the cover to a locked wooden casing. His hands shook with haste as the Sun was set to arrive at any moment. He quickly reached for the master skeleton key in the deep pocket interior of his cape. He always carried it on him as an heirloom to the throne but never found a reason for its use until this moment. He inserted the key into its lock. "Presto!" he said as it snapped open.

He carefully unlatched the case and untombed the book of *Mystical Prophecy*. It was a forbidden book, and any mystic who read it would suffer a grave fate. But he was the Night, one of darkness, privileged to read it — the only one who could read it without paying the price. He never knew why that was, nor was it explained to him. So he questioned whether it was because he came from darkness and maybe one of darkness could reason with such knowledge. But Night wasn't of true darkness; he was a Good Night of light. So he chose not to read it in times past, fearing his goodness would be compromised by what the book would reveal. The Sun, fearing the same, declared it an act of treason if anyone from her court was caught reading the book.

So, Night hid the book in the Divine Clocktower, never tempted to read it until the current hour.

In its case, the book lay dormant in the dullest lackluster of gold with etching barely shown. He debated activating it, but the Clocktower door creaked open. He struggled to lock the wooden casing hearing the Sun run up the stairs. Then she entered the den in her graceful golden light, almost floating off the ground. He quickly covered the book, throwing his cape on it as she ran straight into his arms and embraced him tightly.

"I heard you were ill. How are you? My love." Said the Sun in her warmth.

He looked at her with intense guilt. He had never kept anything hidden and said, "I'm fine. The illness was mild; you don't have to worry about me."

She put her hands on each side of his face and looked into his eyes. They scrunched and tilted with worry, revealing what she feared. "You are lying to me. Something is wrong and I can sense it. Please don't keep me in the dark."

He pulled away from her warm embrace and walked toward the book. "We are connected, of course, you would feel what I feel, and you are right — something is wrong, but I'm not exactly sure. So I thought I would try to figure it out." Night tugged on his cape, revealing the book.

"What is that?" The Sun peered.

"It is the book of *Mystical Prophecy*. Our fates lay in that book."

The Sun became troubled by the sight of the book. "No! Put it away. It's forbidden. It is an act of treason to read it and you know that."

"You, not me, forbid it. It is an act of treason in your court, not mine. I guess there are certain benefits to being one of darkness, so why not reap them?"

Unsettled, the Sun argued. "Do you want to taint your thoughts? Create a worry for yourself in knowing what the future may or may not hold. We discussed this, and I thought we agreed. The answers you seek won't be in that book."

"I have to believe the book was created for a reason. Being that I, the almighty Night, am the only one that can read it without repercussions suggests that I have to read it. It won't have any ill effects over my reign."

"But why? Why do you want to read such a thing now? It hasn't interested you in the past. Are you that worried about your brother? Do you really think he will want to take over your reign?" Said the Sun.

The Night turned to her. "That is one of my main concerns. Yes. I love my brother dearly and I don't want a war with my own brother. But if it means the Dark Ages are returning… I shouldn't speak of such things until I read the book." He then put his hands on her waist and softly said, "All I ask is that you trust my decision. There is not one thing that can deter me from my will or my love for you."

"My Good Night, you don't need the book, but I respect and trust your judgment. Do you remember our pact? When you fall, I rise."

"Until the end of time, my Sun Queen."

Then the Divine Clock chimed in crystal singing bells.

"Well, that's our cue, shall we?" The Sun curtsied to the Night, putting the topic of the forbidden book to rest.

The Night became happy to shift the subject to a better matter — the eclipse. He smiled with joy. "I believe the Black Moon eclipse is upon us, which means it is my turn to take the lead."

He then led her by the hand to the crystalized grounds, where they waltzed perfectly in step. A royal pitch of darkness rolled over the sky, shifting the Sun to shine like a black diamond. Her glistening light leaned against the classical Night, who led her hand to twirl. Shouts of *Bravo!* Echoed through the skyways. *To the Night and the Sun, the perfect union as one!* They toasted. The Sun and the Night waltzed until the Divine Clock separated the two once more.

The Return Home

After reporting to Night to what he deemed a successful mission of whisper delivery, the Greatest Wind headed to his post, high in the heavens. As he looked around, everything remained as he had left it — arctic and hueless — just the way he liked it. He was happy to return to his duty serving Night, sitting amongst the Gods and Goddesses of the round table. He was proud to be part of Night's regal empire and call it home. Yet as time passed, he began to realize as magnificent as Night's court was — it wasn't enchanting.

Without the Goddess of Desire's whisper seed, he no longer could dream. Destiny, the little girl who came to him and made him laugh while he slept, didn't return. When he flew over Earth — he flew alone. Birds found his chill too cold and too strong to flock around. The wondrous Earth and its music no longer opened up to him.

So when he looked down into the abyss of Night's blank canvas and saw the Goddess of Desire's invitation for the Open Fan Soiree sparkle with stardust, he became stirred. To avoid feeling in any particular manner, he checked in on Night.

Night had been spending most of his time in his study, secretly reading the book of *Mystical Prophecy*. He found it interesting in its layout, for it wasn't in any chronological order that dictated a detailed history. Instead, the pages turned in order of Fates. He opened the orb-lit book, and the pages flapped to the Goddess of Desire's chapter, where he began to read.

The Greatest Wind entered the study. "Sire, may I join you for some company?"

The Night quickly hid the book under a brocade pillow. "Of course, I was just thinking about you. Besides the whisper delivery, we haven't had a chance to speak of your journey. How is the Goddess of Desire?"

The Greatest Wind sat across from the Night and said, "She is well. She had to conjure something special for your chosen one — a whisper seed. It nearly drove me insane with its false illusions."

Intrigued, Night said, "Oh, How so?"

The Greatest Wind didn't want to share his dreams of the little girl named Destiny or how the Earth welcomed him. So he thought of the one thing he found to be strange and said, "When the telescope mapped the rat in the West Village park, I was questioned by an odd Park Lark."

Night promptly stood. "The Lark! The Lark came to you? What did it say or, more so, what did it sing to you?"

"Oh, do you know the Park Lark? It was very nonsensical to tell you the truth."

Dumbstruck by the Greatest Wind's lack of awareness, he scolded him. "There is no such thing as a 'Park' Lark! There is only *the* Lark! So what did *the* Lark say?"

The Greatest Wind tried to piece together his interaction with the Lark, but it didn't make sense to him. "Sire, I'm sorry. I simply can't make it out. He was full of riddles. Who is the Lark? And what do you think he wanted with me?"

For such a subject, Night grabbed his pipe and lit it as he began to speak over the smoky noctilucent clouds that formed. "The Lark is an oracle; some mystics consider the Lark a myth. I would be one too if the Lark didn't come to me when I was a young Night. I played hopscotch in Moon's garden when the Lark came to me. The Lark sang a song about the Sun that I found odd, especially being such a young Night. But the experience stayed with me and urged me to form a powerful union with the Sun that instilled harmony in the Mystical Realm. But that wasn't half of it. Little did I know, I would fall for her and love her until the end of time. It is said that if the Lark comes to you, it is to unlock a great purpose. So did he have anything to say about your mission?"

The Greatest Wind was too embarrassed to let the Night know that the Lark sang to him about Feelings, so he said, "Well, I found it odd that he didn't realize the significance of delivering the whisper seed. All he said was, *Oh, yes, the reason for which you think you are here. The purpose for which you think you are serving.* "What do you think he meant by that?"

Stumped, the Night walked over to his window to clear his head with the view of pitch darkness, but rather than view darkness, he saw what the book prophesied — the Goddess of Desire's invitation that was open to all mystics. He shook his head in disbelief and whispered under his breath, "Reckless. How reckless to open your portal to all mystics, Goddess."

He sighed, knowing that the book of *Mystical Prophecy* was valid in its foretelling, which meant the scales would soon shift. *Unless, Unless, I do something about it.* He turned to the Greatest Wind. "I see the Goddess of Desire is opening up her portal. Are you going to the Open Fan?"

The Greatest Wind winced. "Sire, you know that's not my sort of thing."

"I know my judgment of the Goddess has been harsh in the past, and I may still find her actions to be a bit reckless, but I know she is on the side of goodness. Therefore, you should attend the soiree on my behalf and send her my gratitude for her whisper seed."

"Sire, that is something I just won't do. Please forgive me, but I did as you requested, and I found her to gather a whisper. I choose not to go back to her palace." Said the Greatest Wind heading out of the study.

"She won't wait for you! She will move on, and you will regret it if you don't act now. You must act now!" Said Night with urgency.

Aghast at what the Night possibly knew of his history with the Goddess, the Greatest Wind stopped in his tracks. "Regret is a feeling I don't possess. I'll be fine not going. Good Night, sire."

"But you do possess that Feeling! Amongst the most important one!" Night yelled, trying to cut through the Greatest Wind's stubbornness.

Irritated, the Greatest Wind asked, "And which one is that, sire?"

"Love … My dear wind, all the glory that you have created for yourself, all the solar power that you emanate from your strength, which is as powerful as any God's, and yet you are too afraid to go after what you truly want. Do I have a coward in my presence?" Thus mocked the Night.

The Greatest Wind became further irritated to speak about a subject he was trying to avoid. But out of sole duty, he responded. "No, sire, I'm not a coward. It's not in my nature to be such a fool in love. Winds aren't supposed to carry Feelings; that's why we make great soldiers and messengers."

Then Night changed his tone to a fatherly one. "Don't you understand that possessing Feeling has made you the Greatest Wind. I'm aware that it's not a common trait for winds to carry Feelings. I didn't title you the Greatest Wind because of your strength. I titled you the Greatest Wind because I saw — Love. It stirs within your harshest winds. And whether you want to deny it or not, your love for her made you storm into my court and fight for your title. That impressed me and told me you would stand for goodness. Love would make you stand for goodness. Do you still stand for the greater good?"

The Greatest Wind swiftly responded, "Of course, sire. I stand for goodness and your reign. I am your dutiful Wind."

"Then you will do me the honor of attending the Open Fan Soiree with an open heart. That's an order, and you mustn't be late. Divine Timing won't be on your side. You must be on time."

Conflicted, the Greatest Wind bowed to Night and returned to his post. As he tried to get back to work and manage wind traffic, the invitation kept glimmering, getting his attention. He began to think of her and wondered if Night was right. Was he scared of a mere feeling? Was he a coward not to express Love for the Goddess?

The more he thought about her, without the instinct of resistance — without fighting his feelings — his winds picked up speed. Then he stopped thinking of her and stopped thinking at all. He did something he hadn't done since he was a young Northern Wind — he listened to his heart. And when he did that, his cold front subsided and he found himself in action rather than in thought, heading toward her palace.

When he got close to her portal, the fear of Love lifted. As he searched where to land, she stood perfectly alone on her balcony, emitting her beautiful soft flame that guided him to a safe landing — one without collision.

On the palace grounds, he slowly moved toward her. With each step, he could feel himself reverting to the young Northern Wind that wasn't afraid of Love. But just as he was about to call to her — Darkness struck and sent his billows spinning back for miles. It was a darkness so rich in pitch that he lost sight of the Goddess Desire. He called her, but she didn't hear him. When he finally stood clear in front of her, she could no longer see him. Then unexpectedly, he saw her embrace the Darkest Night and hold his hand as she once held his.

Pain, stronger than a burning whisper seed shot through him. *Just as Night had warned me, I'm too late.* At his lowest altitude, the Greatest Wind drifted aimlessly through Moon's Garden.

"Hey, Sad Eyes! Over here!" called a child, giggling in the distance.

"Destiny! Where have you been? I've missed our tea time." Relieved to see his little friend, he perked up.

Destiny ran towards him with her butterflies following behind. "I've been here. I live here in the garden. Are you here for the Open Fan Soiree?"

"Oh, that's not my sort of thing." Said the Greatest Wind trying to hide his broken heart.

"Then it's best if you stay here in the garden. Besides, how will you find your match with those frowny eyes?" Destiny theatrically threw herself to the ground, and exclaimed, "Woe is me! Woe is me!"

The Greatest Wind began to chuckle.

"That's better! Now you're ready for the soiree." Said Destiny cheerfully.

The Greatest Wind sat on a stump and sulked. "I'm too late. I suppose Divine Timing is not on my side."

"You have something greater on your side. You will see."

"And what would that be, my dear Destiny?"

"Me — you will see! Destiny is on your side and always will be." Then she skipped away with her butterflies nesting in her hair.

"Wait, don't leave me, Destiny!" The Greatest Wind said as she vanished into Moon's garden. He ran after the child, but Destiny was nowhere in sight. When he got to the tiger lily fields, an envelope of the purplest of hue lay under a patch. Curiously, he opened it.

My Dearest Destiny,

I miss you so much. I only hope you know how much I love you, my sweetest girl. Happy Birthday, my beautiful daughter. Until we are united again and play in the fields of everlasting dreams.

Your loving mother, now and always,

Desire

With questions funneling in his head, the Greatest Wind stood charged with emotion. His ferocity became wicked to the wisp and bad to the billow. Then, finally, he stormed off to the one that held all the answers.

Night gasped and shut the book of *Mystical Prophecy*, learning the Greatest Wind was too late. "Oh my dear, Greatest Wind, I'm so sorry. There is nothing I can do to stop him now."

He headed for bed and changed into his constellation cloak and cap. Then tucked his feet into the bed, propped himself on a pillow, and gobbled a spoonful of pie to make his dreams sweet. He opened the book to continue reading, only to close it. "I don't have the stomach to digest any more fates." He said, placing the book on his nightstand, fading to a calm sleep.

Until the Greatest Wind charged into Night's bed-chamber, causing the room to shake.

"Wake up! Wake up!" The Greatest Wind thundered.

Startled Night woke. "My dear, Wind, what has happened?"

"Was the Goddess Desire in bloom with my child when the Tornado came to get me? Was it by your command that the Tornado came to fetch me early?"

Night propped himself up on a high pillow. "Things were different then. The Divine Clock was off; it was not the right time then and unfortunately, it's not the right time now. I'm so sorry for that truth."

"You interfered with the Divine Clock! It wasn't off! Is this how it works? Divine timing is right when you say it's so?" The Greatest Wind rumbled.

The Night grew angry to be questioned in such a manner. "How dare you question me! When I have treated you like a son."

Lost in his rage, the Greatest Wind shuddered. "Is Destiny, my child? Answer me!"

Night hesitated to tell him the truth, which was something Night had just learned from the book. But he thought of what the book prophesied and would rather have the Greatest Wind blame him than blame himself. So he flatly said, "Yes, Destiny is your child."

Feeling betrayed by his master, the Greatest Wind stood brewing in his harshest winds. As his anger caught speed, Night's room began to quake, breaking every object in sight. The Night quickly stood and tried to contain the Greatest Wind, but it was too late. His winds ripped through the room, tossing the book of *Mystical Prophecy* into the fireplace.

Night yelled in wrath. "No! Look what you have done. Look what you have done! How dare you. I cast you out! You are now Fallen! Fallen, I say! Leave at once!"

"Fine! Fallen, I am! I no longer want to serve a Night that claims to be good when he kept a father from his only child. I should have been there. I would have been there!" He dropped in altitude and fled.

Night tried to calm himself. He gazed at the burning book as every page popped like heated kernels exploding into ashes. *Maybe this is for the best. Perhaps this book is cursed! For in knowing the future's fate — I could not stop it.* Then, the rat came to mind. He went to his desk and grabbed his telescope to check in on it. The telescope ran its receptors and tracked the rat to the Under Underground — a world unknown to the human eye. "Perfect, stay perfectly hidden, Harold, my chosen one. Take care of the whisper seed that burns in you, for you possess the last whisper to come from the Goddess of Desire."

June of Roses

Roses ballooned from Moon's garden bursting in every palette, shape and size, which marked the new season — the June of roses.

The Goddess of Desire and the Darkest Night lay on the grass, guessing each floral note that passed.

"That one smells like a toast of champagne; it has to be a Symphony rose." She took off her blindfold.

The Darkest Night grinned as he showed the Goddess of Desire the ribboned-adorned rose that sparkled in shades of gold. "Correct. You are quite the rose connoisseur."

"Of course I am. What do you think the headmistress taught us at Goddess school? How to conquer the Universe?" she said jokingly.

The Darkest Night shook with laughter. He appreciated how the Goddess of Desire always made him laugh, which was something he lacked in his life.

"I've gotten all five correct. Now for my surprise as you promised," said the Goddess of Desire, putting her hand out.

"Ah yes, I do have a special treat," he said as he sat up and took out a decorative box from a picnic basket. "I asked Claude to make us something special to mark this occasion, so he created an assortment of June of Roses macarons.

The Goddess excitedly propped up. "That sounds splendid. Let's see what he crafted."

When the Darkest Night opened the box, macarons blossomed in bright colors. "This looks like summer in a box."

"Ah, I think I'll try the Summer Pixie. Seems perfectly harmless," said the Goddess of Desire, closely assessing the macaron. "Looks like a delicious mixture of lavender and rose jam."

"I'm just learning that appearances are always deceiving with Claude's macarons. But I think I'm going to try the Imperial rose. Hopefully, not too much damage can come from the plum filling." Holding the macaron, he turned to her and said, "Shall we?"

She toasted. "Cheers!"

They both took a bite and immediately closed their eyes in ecstatic sweetness.

"Splendid indeed," said the Darkest Night, unaware that his cheeks, tongue and lips had turned a bright imperial red.

The Goddess of Desire couldn't help but snicker until pixie rose dust spouted from her ears, sprinkling the garden. "Oh my!"

Both convulsed into hysterics by the silly spells of Claude's macarons that were anything but romantic.

"Oh, we have to try the Bubble Rosé. What can go wrong?" the Darkest Night said, chuckling sarcastically.

"Yes, we must." The Goddess of Desire giggled.

They waited a couple of minutes and nothing seemed to happen. So the Darkest Night thought it was the perfect time to make his move and kiss the Goddess. It had been a month of courtship and he hadn't worked up the nerve to kiss her.

The sight of her radiant fire in the moonlight, blushing in roses, melted his nerves. So he leaned in close towards her and just as his lips almost met hers, she opened her mouth like a bullfrog and let out a roaring belching bubble.

"Oh my! Was that me?" the Goddess said as she bubbled over in embarrassment.

Then, belching, bubbles that reflected every color in the garden floated out of the Darkest Night's mouth. "I think the macaron kicked in."

"You think?" She couldn't get a word in edgewise without belching.

Trying to be a gentleman, the Darkest Night contained his laughter. "Well, I did promise you a surprise and Claude has not disappointed."

As the Goddess relieved herself of one last bubble squeak, she coyly remarked, "I must repay you for your splendid surprise. But you first have to get the rose notes right. So come on, it's your turn to put on the blindfold."

"That sounds tempting," the Darkest Night said as he nestled his head on her lap and put on the blindfold.

The Goddess of Desire couldn't help but feel flutters in her belly, taking notice of his dimpled smile. She found him handsome and couldn't help but swoon when he got close to her.

She softly brushed the petals of the mystery rose on his cheeks and forehead. Then she tickled his nose with it. The Darkest Night wondered with the Goddess being so close that maybe it was the right time to kiss her. But being a gentleman, which was something he prided himself to be, meant he needed to be patient and kiss her when he was confident of the right moment. So he focused on the rose scent and began to sniff away. "I sense ... apple wood?"

"Yes, that is correct. Can you name the rose?" asked the Goddess of Desire, sweeping the rose close to his nose.

The Darkest Night continued to take in the rose notes to identify it, but a musky note took over. It was a familiar note but not a common one. It kept getting more pungent as he focused on it. "I am picking up on ... it's coming to me." It was so familiar. Suddenly, the rose note pricked his memory. He jerked and sat up, taking off the blindfold. Disturbed, he exclaimed, "Get that away from me! What is that?"

The Goddess of Desire, stunned by the Darkest Night's reaction, revealed the rose. "It's a simple Star rose. Are you okay?"

The Darkest Night calmed himself. "Yes, of course. I just picked up a bizarre scent. It reminded me of something."

"Do you mind if I ask you what that is? Your reaction was quite strong."

"It's nothing." The Darkest Night said as he sat somberly. "Let's pack it up and resume our date some other time."

The Goddess of Desire took his hand. "I don't want our date to end. Please tell me what troubles you. You know of my darkest hour, which deeply saddens me. Why can't you open up to me with something troubling you? Maybe I can help."

He looked into her amber eyes and sensed he could trust her. "You're right, and I don't want to keep anything hidden from you." The Darkest Night hesitated but then told the Goddess of Desire of his past. "When I was a child, I liked playing and running wild in this garden with my brother. One day, a unique rose caught my eye. I hadn't seen anything like it. It was dark in color with a velveteen exterior. I plucked it straight from its root. It must've not been pleased with me doing that since its thorn pricked me. Its poison shot straight into my vein. It turned out to be — a Delirium rose."

The Goddess gasped. "THE KISS OF DEATH! We studied it in school but never thought it would grow here on sovereign grounds. How are you alive and sane?"

"Mother acted quickly and found a mystic healer to take out the poison. But they remained worried since the Delirium ran in my veins. I was sent to the Black Nebulous to isolate incase I became … well … out of control. It was a horrible time. Everyone watched me like a ticking time bomb, waiting for me to rupture into menace. But I proved them wrong. Even today, when I catch those same stares."

The Goddess of Desire empathized with the Darkest Night, and said, "I think you and I are alike. We both are misfits. Misunderstood by Night and the Mystical Realm."

To change the mood, the Goddess of Desire stood up and took his hand. "Now, for your surprise. Come with me, your majesty," she said with a suspicious smile.

Wild and free, they ran and leaped out of her portal, hand in hand, heading straight to the earthbound lands.

The Darkest Night had yet to travel earthbound, so the Goddess took it upon herself to be his tour guide, leading him straight to the Heart of New York City, away from the Belly, but where the lights were in motion just as their courtship.

"I didn't even know I could shapeshift." The Darkest Night examined himself in human form, wearing a Victorian dinner jacket and trousers.

"Yes, that's one of the benefits of being with me. Must I remind you I am the Goddess of Desire?"

The Darkest Night smiled, then excitedly looked around the city. He had never been so close to it. It was almost unrecognizable. "Where are we?"

"This is the city of lights — the Heart of New York. And I must show you the best way to observe it," she said as she reached for his other hand.

"What are you up to Goddess?" the Darkest Night curiously asked as he let her take his other hand.

"I promised you a surprise." The Goddess of Desire giggled and interlaced her arms together with his. She then directed, "Now lean away from me and look up!"

As childish and awkward as the Darkest Night felt, this was the Goddess of Desire's playground and he wanted to know every aspect, every facet of her world.

"Hold tight! Are you ready?" She pulled back and looked up to Night's sky. "Now spin!" she yelled.

Like children, they spun in circles.

"Faster!" The Goddess exclaimed.

The Darkest Night began to laugh, as he had never found amusement in any form of light, and now they were motioning and tracing all around him.

The Goddess then directed, "Okay, now let go!"

The Goddess of Desire nearly fell over with dizziness, but just as she was about to collapse, the Darkest Night pulled her close to him, knowing it was the right moment, softly kissed her.

The Heart of New York gave its blessing sending up a crescendo of violin strings and piano keys from a near distance. All while its skylights traced — entwined — and bound them. It was a New York moment to remember, a souvenir from the city that seemed to be smiling only at them.

Until, a spark like a burning fuse went SNAP! — POP! And as perfect of a New York moment it was, and gentle and warm as his kiss felt — total darkness took over.

"Blackout!" A New Yorker yelled.

When they both opened their eyes, they stood in complete darkness. The Heart of the city that smiled in lights now lurked at them through its towering peeking silhouette.

"Let me guess, Broadway actors? Were you practicing the scenes?" Interrupted a human local walking his dog.

The Goddess of Desire and the Darkest Night remained stunned by the sudden contrast of the city and could only muster a smile at the man.

"Don't worry. I've been here for every blackout, including the one in 1977. Isn't that right, Brutus?" He handed his bloodhound a biscuit, then parked himself on a bench. "My advice is to sit, drink fine wine and enjoy the show — to the Darkest Night!"

The Darkest Night tipped his hat at the man, enjoying hearing his praise. "That's one for the count," he murmured.

"Did we do this?" said the Goddess of Desire, jarred to see such a dark city.

"I'm more stunned that a local called us Broadway actors. Why do you think he would assume such a thing?" the Darkest Night quipped, brushing his turn-of-the-century coat.

The Goddess of Desire raised her brow. "I'm being quite serious. Is this how we will impact the world?"

The Darkest Night calmly took her hand and said, "I think it's time you let me take the lead and show you exactly what our impact can be." Then he opened his portal. "It's my turn to be the tour guide." A racing chariot waited for them.

The Goddess of Desire hesitated, but as he jumped in the driver's seat and grinned at her with his dimpled smile, she couldn't help but hop on. "Alright then, where are we going?"

He turned to her and jokingly said, "To the Moon!"

Charlie and the Warpers

Charlie woke up at the same time every morning — 6 am. For a mystic barkeep that got home at 5 am, that was unusually early. One hour of sleep was all he needed — sixty minutes — three thousand and six hundred seconds of sleep, which was quite a bit of time to rest for Charlie. It was the one thing that if anyone ever noticed, they would learn his secret. Charlie was a Warper and had come from a long lineage of Warpers, which some mystics would call "time thieves."

But how could anyone suspect when Charlie stayed still in the present moment? For nearly half a century, he had been a barkeep at Desiree's Tavern in Shiner, Texas. He never took a vacation, never left Shiner and he certainly didn't time travel.

When Charlie was born, his father thought it was best to raise Charlie in the present time, and where time ran slow, which led them to Shiner, Texas. *A time that ticks slow allows you to grow*, his father would say. His mother, unfortunately, had the time itch and kept moving along. So his father did his best to raise Charlie and teach him the ways of a time Warper.

Every morning, at the crack of Dawn, his father would take Charlie to the train depot, where they both would sit on a rickety platform, cracking sunflower seeds as they patiently waited for the right portal trains to pass.

"Alright, we've got two freights coming in. What did I teach you, Charlie?"

Charlie spat out sunflower shells onto the tracks and quoted his father's teachings. "When two speeding trains pass each other in opposing directions, you have the perfect time portal."

"That's right, but you have to see it. You have to see where you're going first. You wouldn't just jump on that train without seeing it first." Then his father stood on the platform as the trains came rushing in. "Alright, Focus! Focus Charlie! Do you see it?"

Charlie focused the best he could but could only see the blur of the speeding trains. With angst, Charlie said, "Nope. Nothing Dad."

"That's alright, Charlie; we always have tomorrow. That's the beauty of this town. We always have plenty of time here."

But Charlie became frustrated by the slowness of time and exclaimed, "I should see it by now, Dad! How will I ever be a good Warper if I can't even see the portal?"

"Be patient Charlie, you'll know and it will come when you are ready. I wish it were your Mother teaching you these things. She had the perfect way of explaining it. She would say, *Expand your frame. Set your focus to infinity and expand it.*

"Expand what frame Dad? How do I do that?" Charlie pouted.

"Ok, what do you see all around you? Look around and tell me everything you see."

Charlie began to observe his surroundings and said, "I see you, Dad, right in front of me. I see the blue sky above. I see the railroad sign to the right, the train tracks to the left that head out yonder, and the sunflower shells on the tracks below."

"Alright, everything that you have just described — think of it as your partial frame. It's what your eyes are limiting you from seeing. When you expand your frame, you see it all. You see the workings, the behind-the-scenes, and all the divine clocks. You see the Multiverse."

"The Multiverse!" Charlie exclaimed with wonder. Charlie didn't exactly know what the Multiverse was, but it seemed grand, so he became eager to crack the understanding of a Warper.

Charlie practiced expanding his frame every night until he dropped to sleep. But one morning, when he woke up, an idea came to him. *Of course! That should work.* He rummaged through his drawers and took out an old pair of neon-green framed sunglasses he had found lying between the train tracks one summer day. He put them in his shirt pocket, ready to see The Multiverse.

In a cowboy stance, wearing his neon-green sunglasses, Charlie stood on the platform waiting for the right trains to pass.

"That's good, Charlie; everyone has their unique way of seeing it. The sunglasses just might be your thing!" said his father enthusiastically.

The train tracks abruptly began to tremble. Charlie's father took out his binoculars to see what was coming in. "Charlie, two bullet trains are coming our way. Remember, when they cross, try to focus on infinity and expand your frame."

The freight trains came charging at one another like raging bulls steaming in speed. Charlie locked his focus to infinity, which minimized the blur of speed, then he expanded his frame beyond his sunglasses and when the trains crossed each other, something clicked, and the time portal slid open. Charlie saw it — he saw the Multiverse and it glinted in its brass maze. It was grander than anything he had imagined it to be — grander than his life in Shiner or even he.

"Whoa!" Charlie cried in amazement.

"Do you see it, Charlie?" his father asked.

"I see it, Dad!!! I see it!" Charlie now knew without a doubt that he was a Warper.

On the day he turned eighteen, his father had to be sure whether Charlie wanted to live the life of a Warper and asked the pending question. "Son, the day has come. Are you sure you want to jump that train today and join your mother and me in the Multiverse? It's quite alright if you choose not to. When I was your age, it was too much, too grand for me to handle, and I wish I had the choice I'm giving you now."

The grander, the better! Charlie thought. The great Multiverse was calling, and there was nothing to stop him, so without mulling it over, he said, "I'll jump the train with you, Dad. Besides, I have to figure it out on my own."

So the following day, they headed to the train depot, cracked some sunflower seeds and waited.

"Okay, our trains are coming in. Remember, you must see it before jumping that train. Okay, Charlie? Let me know when you see it!"

Charlie put on his sunglasses and expanded his frame until the maze of the Multiverse opened up to him. "Alright, Dad, I see it!"

So proud of his son, he said, "That's just great, Charlie. Do you see your mother waving at us to the left?"

Charlie turned his gaze and saw his mother surrounded by winding wheels of time. She waved at Charlie with tears in her eyes. Charlie became emotional and began tearing up, "Yes, I see her, Dad."

"Okay, Charlie, it's time. We need to jump this train."

Both leaped from the platform into the Workings room, where Charlie ran straight into his mother's arms.

"My son!" His mother held him tightly.

His father joined in on the hug as they all stood reunited.

"Where are we?" Charlie asked as he looked around the industrial room.

"This is the Workings, where all time activity is trafficked for clearance by the Time Tockers. This is where it all begins. Where you will learn how to play the maze."

"Do I have the ability to speed, slow, and change time?" asked Charlie.

"Yes, but you have to work with the Time Tockers. Otherwise, you will be a time thief, and we're not a family of time thieves," said his mother firmly.

"So there's more to learn before I can time travel?" Charlie pouted.

"Charlie, you need to be patient. It's a lot to take in," said his father.

"That's quite okay, I understand, Charlie," said his mother. "I was like you, very eager and impatient. Some say it was the time itch in me. But the Multiverse can be very tricky, so it's important to fully know and understand its maze before getting caught up in it."

So the next day, Charlie reported to the Time Tockers where he began to learn the rules of changing time.

"As you know, we are Warpers. To describe our purpose, we record, fast forward, rewind and restore. We are the only ones who can move things around and change time, but we must be careful when doing it. Otherwise, things can get out of order. When we make a move, it's like playing a game of chess. You have to think three steps ahead," said the Time Tocker.

"What if you make a wrong move?" wondered Charlie.

"It's not whether you make a wrong move because we all sometimes make mistakes, it's how you correct them and unfortunately, you have to do it fast. You have to cancel, clear and delete your mistake before it creates change in the world. But don't worry, practice makes perfect and you will *slowly* come to learn."

There was that word again, that word Charlie came to despise — SLOW. Charlie sighed, now wondering how long it would take to time travel. He was ready; he understood that all he needed to be was careful about his steps and missteps. Every morning on the way to report to the Workings room, the Multiverse maze called to him with its brass luster of wonder, which made it hard not to step into it.

One evening, after a week of training sessions with the Time Tockers, Charlie got the time itch and without thinking, he leapt into the first Multiverse room he saw.

He landed in the natural world of the roaring 1920s, where Charlie found himself standing on a performing stage while silent faces waited for him to entertain them. He stiffened up, not knowing how to get out of the situation where the spotlight was on him.

With fright in his eyes, he turned to a frantic stage manager who was shuffling dancers off stage, then looked at Charlie with a raised brow and yelled, "Go on! Move your feet!"

Charlie didn't know what to do exactly or how to do it, but he did as the stage manager said and took a step. But his shoe wobbled, so when he glanced at the souls, he realized they were hooved just like the horses in Shiner.

"Tap! Tap those feet!" someone yelled.

Charlie began to sweat under pressure, but when he struck his foot, something magical happened — his feet came to life. He jumped, leaped, and scuffled to the rhythm of his tapping feet. This experience exhilarated Charlie and with the popping sounds of horns and the hand claps of applause — his time itch grew.

Every evening he continued to jump into the various rooms in the Multiverse, finding excitement in the unknown waiting to be discovered. He had jumped into an 80s room, where he got to play video games at an arcade all night. Then went onto the next room where he crashed a royal wedding in the 1700s at the court of Versailles. Charlie was becoming a time thief and thought he could get away with it if he were careful enough.

One evening after dinner with his parents, a different part of the maze caught his eye. It wasn't like the other rooms; it glowed in soft light and captivated him to leap right in.

He landed in Moon's Garden and knew he wasn't in the natural world judging by the air pressure. *The mystical realm? How odd.* He thought as he wasn't aware that Warpers had any access to it. He strolled through the various luminous gardens in full bloom and decided to nap near the rose garden that drifted with sweet rose notes. After his nap, he got hungry, so he checked his shirt pocket and found sunflower seeds. "Wow! I forgot I had these." He said as he began to crack and pop them into his mouth. Unnoticed, a sunflower seed escaped his hand and fell into the rose bushes. When he got up to head back, he retracted his steps and cleaned up. *There, all restored! I didn't even leave an imprint on the grass.* He thought. But the sunflower seed that fell in the rose bush remained unseen and slowly began sinking into the soil.

Little did Charlie know that the foreign earthbound seed planted in sovereign grounds would cause a disruption — a Delirium rose would spout. A Delirium rose that would prick the Darkest Night as a child.

When the Time Tockers tracked Charlie, it was too late. He could not change or restore what he had done. The Darkest Night, a royal, was pricked by the Delirium rose. Charlie was immediately arrested and tried by a jury of Tockers. There had never been such a scandal in the history of Warpers and nobody quite knew what to do or how to fix it.

"If Night gets word of this, he will hang us all for treason. It's bad enough that most from the Mystical Realm label all of us as Time Thieves." Said the Time Tocker judge.

"Please, your honor, he is my son. I can reassure you this was all a mistake," cried Charlie's mother.

"There is no doubt this was a mistake, but it was a mistake that was overlooked. A mistake that wasn't restored. A careless mistake that could cost us our existence if any word of this gets out!" the Time Tocker judge exclaimed.

"But they don't have to know. Nobody has to know. Punish me. I should have known he had the time itch," his father pleaded.

The judge then turned his gaze towards Charlie. "Did anyone see you, Charlie?"

Charlie's freckles turned to splotches feeling guilty for what he had done. With his head down, he answered, "No, your honor. No one was in the garden. I'm sorry for being so reckless, but it is my fault and no one else is to blame other than myself."

The judge then addressed the court. "I will have to work with the other Time Tockers to make sure word of this never gets out. So let's rest on this issue for now." Then he turned to Charlie. "I will discuss your sentence with your parents. Until then, you will stay in the Workings room where the Time Tockers will keep a watch on you."

Charlie couldn't raise his head and face everyone. In shame, he kept it down and said, "Yes, your honor."

The following day, his mother and father flew into the Workings room.

"Mom, Dad!" He cried as he ran into their arms.

"I'm so sorry, Charlie, you inherited the time itch from me. I wish you would have told me you had it. I could've helped you," cried his mother.

"I didn't even know what it was, but I understand now, Mom. I understand why you left Dad and me in Shiner — you couldn't keep still." Tears streamed down Charlie's face.

Trying to be strong for his son, his father firmly said, "Charlie, we have to hand down your sentence. Just know it's for your own good."

Charlie pulled himself away from the clutches of his mother's arms and said, "I'm ready. Anything is better than this shame."

Both his mother and father walked Charlie to a room in the Multiverse maze, where the brightest of white light spilled over from every corner.

"This is where we leave you, Charlie. You need to jump into this room," said his mother sobbing in tears.

Charlie took a few steps into the light-filled room and looked back at his parents. Then, with a simple wave, he said his goodbye. Charlie leaped towards his fate — his sentence. He felt himself falling, changing, fading and then it all went blank.

When Charlie woke up, to his surprise, he was an infant — reborn into the same life. He was still Charlie and had the same mother and father, but time had rewound. One might think, *Not such a bad sentence*, but Charlie still had his memory. He would vent. *It's a prison sentence, alright, having an eighteen-year-old brain in a doughy baby body.* But it taught him patience. It led him to retrace every step, not to change the future, but keep perfectly still.

After a while, things got better for Charlie as he began to walk, talk, and eat solid foods. His best day was when his father took him to the train depot, where they ate breakfast burritos, one change Charlie enforced in his new recycled life: *No sunflower seeds!*

Then the cycle of his life began again just as he remembered it.

"When two opposing trains at fast speeds pass each other, you have the perfect portal. But you have to see where you're going. It won't lead you anywhere if you can't see the portal. So you have to see it," said his father, teaching him how to be a Warper.

Charlie reenacted his conversation with his father the best he could remember it, not wanting to change a single thing. Too scared of the consequences, he counted until his eighteenth birthday — his freedom day. The day he would make a different choice.

When the time finally came, his father asked him, "Son, I want to give you a choice my parents never gave me. Today, will you join your mother and me in the Multiverse, or do you want to live a normal life here in the natural world?"

Charlie stood on the platform thinking, *How wonderful of a life it can be to do things over and time travel with my family*. After all, he didn't see the harm in going back knowing what he did. *This time it can be different!* "Yes, Dad, I'll jump the train with you."

His father's eyes gleamed with joy, "So proud of you, Charlie. Your mother will be happy to see you." Then his father took out his binoculars. "Alright, get your sunglasses ready. Our trains are coming in and taking us home."

Charlie stood in his cowboy stance, wearing sunglasses as he did in his previous life, but just as the train tracks began to tremble, so did Charlie. He could feel the time itch stirring, tempting him to thieve. His mind accelerated in speed, and when his frame expanded through the bullet trains, he didn't see his mother waving to him from the Workings room as he did before. Instead, he saw all the inviting rooms of the wondrous brass maze calling him.

His father jumped into the portal, "Come on, Charlie, it's your turn! Jump!" He yelled.

Charlie took off his sunglasses and tears rolled. "I'm sorry, Dad, I can't." Charlie chose to stay behind — too scared to make the same mistake.

His father could only smile and bow his head at Charlie to reassure him it was okay. Then as the portal shut, he could hear the faint voice of his father saying, "I'm still proud of you, Charlie. We love you."

THE NIGHT'S FABLE

After hours of sitting blankly on the platform, Charlie dusted himself off and headed back into town. When he saw a sign hanging from a window that read, *Barkeep Needed*, he decided that would be his calling to his new life.

He thought of his family every morning when he picked up his breakfast burrito and ate it at the train depot. He sometimes would hear the voices of the other Warpers, drifters, and time thieves as they passed by. He enjoyed it when they would send a message from home.

"Your family says they love you! Come visit!"

All Charlie could do was raise his hand as they passed by. He never was fast enough to say anything back.

Time continued to pass, and Charlie kept still. Then time began to pass him by and the ever-changing world began to move fastly around him as he continued to stay still. He saw humans and mystics come and go. He saw them change and grow, and yet he stayed still. Finally, it was time for Charlie to start moving again.

One morning at the train depot, Charlie took out his sunglasses and began fiddling with them. He was interrupted by a drifting Warper.

"You can't stay still forever! You need to jump that train!"

Charlie took it as advice and knew the voice was right. So he packed up and decided he would jump the train again. But just as he closed his bar and put the last bar stool on the counter, the Greatest Wind stepped into *Desiree's Tavern* in complete despair.

"Well, well, what brings you back here? I thought Maestro would have spit you out somewhere." Said Charlie.

"I've been cast out from Night's court. I'm now Fallen. Got any work for me?" Said the Greatest Wind.

Charlie could tell the Greatest Wind wasn't in the best shape. So he opened up the bar and decided not to jump the train for at least a little longer. After all, it wouldn't be very Texas-like not to help a friend.

Little did Charlie know that his sentence would be lifted by that act of kindness and sacrifice towards someone from Night's court, where the Delirium rose was still growing. After that, he wouldn't have to jump the train to start moving again. Instead, something bigger would lead him to it.

The Sun's Jubilee

From the east, west, north, and south — toasts, boasts, spills, and oaths rippled from mystics in every skyway waiting to enter the procession portal to honor the Sun on her Golden Jubilee. This occurrence, when the Divine Clock reset itself to the sundial of the Sun, marked a special day that not only celebrated the Sun Queen but that brought unity to the Mystical Realm. It was the only time of the season when both, the Sun and the Night courts could join joyously.

Soldiers of Order marched towards the skyway borders and waited for the clock's countdown before unlocking the portal.

Mystics counted and chanted:

At Ten, the queen gets her hen!

At Nine, she rises and shines!

At Eight, Never late!

At Seven, The Queen dances in heaven!

At Six, Her sundial ticks!

At Five, She comes alive!

At Four, She hits the floor!

At Three, She will always be!

Two, The queen to see!

One, On her Golden Jubilee!

With twists and dials, the Soldiers of Order unlocked the procession portal. The rush of mystics in high spirits gathered around the golden skyway that led to the Divine Clock, where the Sun would set and sit alongside Night. The bright sounds of royal trumpets let out warm melodies of the Sun's anthem — A Perfect Day. And a perfect day, it all seemingly began.

The Sun rose in her sunroom while her ladies needled around her getting her dressed.

"You look magnificent, your majesty. You are ready." Said the Sun's head lady-in-waiting after placing one last sunbeam on the Sun Queen's dress.

"Thank you, Lady Citrine." Then she turned to address the rest of her ladies. "Thank you all for your service on such a chaotic day. Please make your way to your chariots, and I will see you at… well… the thing."

Her ladies burst into laughter.

"You are too modest, your majesty. It is your day and we are so grateful to be part of it. Please take a minute to take it in." So said Lady Citrine as she curtsied and followed the frenzy of excitement leading outside the court.

While the Sun waited for her chariot, she glanced at herself in the mirror and took notice of her crown that gleamed perfectly, her gown that draped perfectly, and even her jewels that sparkled ever so perfectly. Her reflection from head to toe was one of sheer perfection. She began to practice her twirl for the finale waltz with Night when suddenly a sunbeam fell off her dress. It didn't look like the other beams; it was dim and lackluster. Without paying much attention, she picked it up and placed it back on her dress. When she caught its flare in the mirror, her mind raced with Curiosity.

She became very Curious to know what was in the book of *Mystical Prophecy*. She had been troubled with Curiosity since Night mentioned he was planning on reading it. *The Night grows as he knows more than I. He now holds the power of wisdom over me. I need to know what he knows. I need to read that book!* She hastily thought, *If I escape now, I will have enough time to get to it.*

Then a knock on the door interrupted her reverie.

"Your majesty, your chariot awaits you." Said her footman.

"Yes, of course. I'll be out in a minute." She took one last glance in the mirror and noticed her cheeks pale in color, so she began pinching them to bronze. Curiosity came rushing again. *I need to know what the Night knows.* But then, her brightness dimmed and the mirror reflected all the fine lines her golden shine hid.

"Wrinkles from the Divine Time! What a birthday gift!"

The footman knocked again, "Your majesty, is everything alright? It is time."

She stepped away from the mirror and didn't want to glance into it again. *It's Curiosity causing such dimness. I won't be fooled by its spell.* She told herself. So she cleared her mind and thought of nothing but her golden light. *I am the Sun! I am the Golden Star! I won't let this Curiosity get very far.*

Outside her court, chariots lined in various shapes and themes, waiting to head towards the procession.

Dawn, the Sun's younger sister, tried to regain her composure as she couldn't help but yawn from all the waiting. "I thought we were riding on my watch?" Dawn yelled from her chariot window. "Don't blame me if I'm a fumbling spawn of yawns today."

Sunshine, the Sun's top commander, sat across from Dawn, irritated by her lack of etiquette. "Dawn, your highness, please try to control it. It's infectious."

Frustrated, Dawn exclaimed, "I'm trying to! Maybe your Cleaner can do something about it?"

Ray, a.k.a. "The Cleaner," was a peculiar southern ray of light who stuck out everywhere he went due to his hair, a mullet of light strands. Even though Ray wasn't of royalty and he had an unusual sense of shiny style, Sunshine recognized that he had a knack — a gift. Ray could turn any bad situation to good — rain to a rainbow — a dark cloudy day to a happy sunshiny one. So when Sunshine realized a yawning problem needed cleaning, he quickly looked for Ray in the lineup of chariots.

I bet he's in there. Thought Sunshine when a chariot of blinking LED lights caught his eye. Sure enough, when Sunshine peeked into the chariot, Ray was getting his hair braided by the Festival Goddesses of Light.

"Have I seen you at any of the desert festivals, Ray?" wondered Lampetia, thinking the southern ray of light looked familiar.

Ray smugly smiled as he couldn't believe he was getting such attention. "No, ma'am, my work hasn't led me to the desert lands yet."

"What is it that you do for your line of work, Ray?" asked another Festival Goddess.

Sunshine, trying to get his attention away from the Goddesses of Light, found himself in repetition, "Ray… Ray… Ray… Ray!" he called.

Startled to see his commander sneering at him, Ray stiffened to a soldier's sitting position. "Yes, sir. Sorry, didn't see you there, sir."

Sunshine dismissed the odd scene and got straight to the point. "We have a cleaning situation. Dawn, the royal highness, can't stop yawning. It's quite infectious. It might ruin the perfect day set for the Sun's Jubilee. Is there anything you can do about it?"

"Hmmm, some yawnin' that needs some fixin', huh? I might have the right fix for that." Ray took out several flasks from his jacket and began to juggle, mix and pour his specialty shine into a light shaker.

THE NIGHT'S FABLE

The Goddesses of Light watched Ray work his magic. "Oh, you're a cleaner! We could have used your talent at that dreadful Fire Festival," said one of the Goddesses as she marveled while he worked his magic.

Ray, trying to make an impression with the ladies, said, "Goddesses, I like to consider myself a shine-ologist. I make things real shiny and nice."

Sunshine rolled his eyes at the display of showmanship. But in no time, Ray had the anti-yawning cocktail.

"I like to call this my Spirit Juice. It should stop the yawnin' and pep that royal highness right up."

"Oh, no, Ray. We don't need the royal highness 'pepped up.' Dawn is best when she is calm. Trust me."

"No problemo! Sir." Ray took out another flask marked Moonshine - *The Real Stuff*, then added two drops of it into the drink. "Here you go, sir; this should do the trick."

"Alright, let's hope!" said Sunshine. Then he took the special drink over to Dawn, who drank it immediately and became rid of her yawns.

The perfect day became restored and the chariots waited patiently for their Sun Queen.

When the Sun stepped out of her court, her footman stood holding her chariot door open, but rather than step into the chariot, she called for her lion.

"Leo, come!" She then turned to the footman. "I will lead with my strength today!"

The footman bowed to his Queen, "Yes, your majesty, I will let the procession leaders know you are on your way."

Her lion roared while she stood victoriously leading the procession — reigning with one hand — waving graciously to the crowds with the other.

Mystics waved their sun-crested flags, all trying to catch a glimpse of the rising Sun. Finally, at the crossway of the golden skyway, the Sun and her court halted where Night and his court waited to join the procession line up. Shouts of *Bravo!* Echoed as Night and his court stepped out of the glistening darkness and into the light of day.

Night bowed to his Sun Queen. "My love, you look radiant as ever. But, unfortunately, I can only bear your beauty for a few seconds. So if you don't mind …" He squinted and placed black sun shades over his eyes.

She gleamed with happiness as his silly humor put her mind at ease. *The book has not turned him.* She thought. "Thank you, my king. The brightest days could not exist without the tranquility of a Good Night. I welcome you and your nocturnal court into my light." Then the Sun rose as her lion roared and stood on its hind legs. "To unity!"

Floods of overflowing cheer showered over her as she gallantly led the procession to the throne. And by the time she sat on her throne alongside Night, she was back to herself again — a strong, confident Sun Queen.

Morning stars shot into the sky, spreading more light of Good Day. The festivities in her honor were on their way. But it was between the musical act of Harry Sparkles and the dance choreography of the Royal Sun Family when the dim sunbeam fell from her dress and glinted onto her from the ground. Curiosity returned to the Sun's mind. She casually turned to the Night. "So, did the book reveal anything of interest?"

Distracted by the excitement of the musical stars, Night replied tepidly, "What book?"

Irritated, she poked him. "You know which book I'm referring to."

"Don't concern yourself with such things, especially on your day, my love. Please enjoy it. Surprisingly, I certainly am." The Night turned his attention back to the viewing stage.

But the Sun couldn't contain Curiosity. She needed to know what was in the book. While applauding the performers on stage, she nonchalantly said, "At some point, you will reveal to me what is in that book?"

The Night ignored her and bobbed his head to the music.

This upset the Sun, and she lost her sense of calm. "Why won't you answer me!"

Shocked to see the Sun in such dim light, he tried to reason with her. "My love, it is I, the Night, the dark one here, telling *you*, the Sun, to *lighten up!* So for me and all that are here for you, will you do just that?"

Appalled to be spoken to in that manner, she sat back quietly, scorching.

The Night, noticing that her light remained dim, continued. "Please, my love, don't fester. Show your light. Your smile will do that for you. Just smile."

She boiled. *How dare he Night-splain me. I must certainly read the book now.*

Then the Sun noticed the Night was about to speak again but before he could get a word in, she sarcastically sniped. "Yes, my ki*ng, I'm* 'smiling' Soak it up!"

Gossip could sense salacious news was brewing, so she swiveled through the royal seating area and sneakily stood behind the Sun and the Night and with a patient ear waited for something newsworthy to unfold.

The Ring of Fire

The Goddess of Desire found it strange to be back in Night's heavens enjoying herself. After all, she took pride in being an earthbound goddess, but here she was with the Darkest Night, reminding her of the place she once called home.

Night drove into a food drive-thru of orbiting arches.

"*Craters*! It's still here and just as I remember it to be." Said the Goddess of Desire, peering at the menu.

The Darkest Night spoke loudly into the transmitting speaker. "We will have two crater taters, two blackened Night burgers... and...." He turned to the Goddess. "Anything else to add?"

"Do they still carry the drink named after me? My fire-cream soda?"

The Darkest Night then added, "And two Desires, please."

In a digitized voice, the attendant responded, "Coming right up, sir."

The Goddess of Desire sat humbled that even when she cursed Night's skies, wanting to forget where she came from, the skies never forgot her and continued to honor her name.

A siphon of tentacles shot out a variety of space food into their chariot.

"This blackened burger is new. I've never had anything like this. It's almost human-like food. How can this grow here?" asked the Goddess, guzzling her fire soda.

"Ah, yes, this is my doing. Moon's not the only one who gardens. Your burger is filled with vegetation grown from my own garden. I think it's important to be self-sustaining and that's how I reign the Black Nebulous."

"I'm impressed. I would love to see it. Can we go there next?"

"I have a better idea. You know the Sun's Jubilee is taking place at this very moment?"

With a mouth full of burger, the Goddess of Desire muttered, "Is this your way of buttering me up to go?"

"Maybe…" said the Darkest Night with a persuasive smile.

The Goddess of Desire didn't have a good feeling about the idea. "I don't think I'm ready to face Night at such a grandiose event, with both courts in attendance. He didn't even attend my Soiree. I know he harbors resentment towards me."

Trying to convince the Goddess, the Darkest Night reminded her. "You left a grand impression on the Mystical Realm from being a gracious hostess at your Open Fan Soiree. It would be a delight for everyone else, other than Night, to see you again."

"I just want it to be you and I at the moment. Can we please not go?" The Goddess of Desire sulked in her crater taters.

"Well, I do have to deliver my gift to the Sun and I was hoping you could help me with that. If you come with me, I promise we will only be spectators watching from a distance." He leaned in and grabbed her hand. "It will be just you and I."

Persuaded by his smile, she said, "Fine, for you and my Sun Queen, I'll go. But only as a spectator."

"Of course." The Darkest Night slurped his soda, giddy in a secret plan.

Gossip was determined to find some exciting news to report, so with a prying eye, her telescopic lens scoured every skyway, stage, and mystic and honed in on every conversation at the Sun's Jubilee. But to her disappointment, it was a Good Day, free of any disorder. But then, her telescope led her to the Clocktower, where it spotted the Darkest Night and the Goddess of Desire watching the festivities from a distance.

Gossip coyly whispered in the Sun's ear, "Isn't that your brother-in-law with… her?" Then handed the Sun her telescope.

Knowing Gossip liked to stir trouble, the Sun tried to refrain from reacting. Instead, in a subdued tone, she said, "Yes, I did invite the Darkest Night. I would like to think my Jubilee represents unity and is the perfect time for all families to come together."

"You did what? You invited who?" The Night became upset as he looked through his telescope and noticed the Darkest Night waving at him from the Clocktower. "Well, that's just lovely. Both of them openly joined at the hip — what a pair they're going to make."

Forgetting Gossip was standing behind her, the Sun scorned, "And how would you know what type of pair they will make? Maybe if you would share what you know, I, the Sun, the one of light here, wouldn't feel so kept in the dark."

Gossip devilishly smirked, knowing she wouldn't have to do much stirring. She could sense something newsworthy was about to break — something EXCLUSIVE, and she was going to make sure she was on top of it.

At that moment, the Sun's footman delivered a black envelope. "From the Darkest Night, your majesty."

"Oh great, what now?" The Night said bleakly.

When the Sun read the note, she didn't think much of it, being distracted by Curiosity.

THE NIGHT'S FABLE

My Queen, Happy Birthday.

When the bells ring, I urge you to look up into the bright blue sky, for I have a present for you in your honor.

Your loving brother-in-law

- The Darkest

"What is it?" the Night asked.

The Sun handed the note to Night.

After reading it, the Night alerted his men to be on the watch. Then turned to the Sun, "I can assure you, he is up to something."

"You clearly have strong animosity towards your brother and I don't see the same coming from him. Are you sure he is up to something?" Said the Sun while observing the Darkest Night through her telescope. "He seems to be enjoying himself with the Goddess of Desire."

Night slumped over his throne, disturbed. "I didn't realize it seemed like I had animosity towards him. Frustrated? Yes. Irritated by his actions? Absolutely. But to have such strong animosity towards him is something I don't want to have towards my own brother."

The Sun urged Night. "Then please let go of this idea that he's trying to take over your reign. Have faith that it won't happen and if his actions irritate you, then simply 'smile' just as you advised me to do."

The Night chortled. "Touché! My love, I'm beginning to realize that this day has brought mirrors before us. To show us what we are reflecting — to test us with it." Then he grabbed her hand and kissed it.

"There you are, the Night I know and love. The wise Night — My Good Night," she said as she returned his kiss.

Gossip projected the Sun and the Night's affection onto the screen above the viewing stage. "The Night and the Sun, perfect union as one!" Cheered from the skyways.

The Sun, blushing from the applause, rose from her seat and waved to the skyways. Then the Night stood behind her and twirled her to appease the crowds further. Shouts of *Bravo!* Echoed.

The Darkest Night peering at the Sun, put down his telescope. "That's our cue!" He excitedly said, taking the Goddess of Desire's hand and leading her to the crystalline grounds. "It's time to present our gift to the Sun."

"You seem awfully excited about this. What are we doing exactly?" asked the Goddess of Desire.

The Darkest Night looked towards the Black Nebulous in the far dark distance. Then with a snap of his fingers, a spotlight cast over them.

"Goddess of Desire, will you do me the honor of dancing with me?" He bowed to her.

Squinting from the bright spotlight, she worried, "Here? On the Divine Clock grounds? But that will cause an eclipse. Are you sure the Sun will see this as a gift?"

"In the Heart of New York, during its blackout moment, you were concerned over our impact together. If you truly want to know what that impact can be, you will dance with me." Said the Darkest Night.

Even though the Goddess of Desire swooned at the romantic gesture, she pondered if it was a good idea to cause such an unexpected eclipse or, worse, a disastrous one. But then, a tambourine jingled, followed by the deep vibrations of bass that fell against the slow flicks of the mamba drums. *This music doesn't seem like any ordinary waltz music.* She thought, swaying her hips. The Darkest Night held out his hand, but she continued to be cautious, slowly moving around him as the music rattled. Finally, the rock band from the Black Nebulous, realizing the two weren't in sync, changed the rhythm to meteor rockabilly. Feverishly the Goddess began to tap her feet and when the Darkest Night reached for her hand again, she took a chance and grabbed it.

A rolling pitch of darkness took over the bright blue sky, which got the attention of the crowds thinking it was part of the grand finale. All took out their magical telescopes and looked towards the heavens. And just as they did, the Darkest Night wrapped his hands around the Goddess of Desire and swung her high and low. Sparks of fireworks lit up the dark sky. Then he twirled her spinning into a Ring of Fire eclipse.

Shouts of *Bravo!* Echoed. "To the Darkest Night and the Goddess of Desire! A power couple!" The two that stood alone as misfits dazzled together, mystifying the Mystical Realm.

Gossip snidely remarked, "Has someone outshined the Sun?"

Snickers and giggles swept through the crowds, which triggered the Sun. Abruptly she excused herself.

"Where are you going?" asked the Night.

"I just need to shine my nose before the finale, if you don't mind. I'll be right back." Said the Sun as she hurried off towards the Clocktower. It was her chance to get to the book while everyone remained distracted by the Darkest Night and the Goddess of Desire's performance.

The Sun swung open the tower door, then ran up the spiraling stairs, and there, openly on the same chair where Night showed her the book, it lay. She didn't think to wonder how odd it was for a forbidden book to be openly displayed. Instead, she sat and began to flip through its pages, hoping to put her Curiosity at rest. Her finger drew to a particular page that lit up as she read:

The prick of the Delirium Rose will slowly grow, not only in the Darkest of Nights but in every God and Goddess. When the rose pricked, it pricked them all.

Troubled, the Sun exclaimed, "It is the Delirium Rose! It's growing in me and affecting me with Curiosity and killing my faith. It's growing in all of us. I must warn Night! Or does he know this already?"

But before the Sun could warn Night, Gossip stood above the staircase looking down at the Sun and called, "Treason! Treason! Treason on you!" Gossip had witnessed the Sun read the forbidden book.

The Sun tried to quiet the chatter. "Gossip, calm down. It is a forbidden book by the rule of my own thumb and I can choose to overrule it."

"You can't overrule it, your majesty. It is written in the laws. Aren't you embarrassed to go against your convictions? And now you want me to turn a blind eye? What kind of ruler are you? Treason! Treason! Treason on you!" Wailed Gossip.

This got the attention of the Guards of Order who stormed in and when they learned of the treacherous act, arrested the Sun Queen immediately. Night and the Sun's court broke into pandemonium when word of the occurrence got out and ran straight to the Clocktower to support the Sun. But it was too late. The Guards of Order had locked up the Sun in the Tower chamber.

"This is preposterous! Release her at once!" Night commanded. "I can assure you that the book she read is a fake. It was placed there purposely as a trap. The original book no longer exists and I know this because I witnessed it burn. Release her now!"

But then the Darkest Night stepped in. "Oh, I can assure *you*, dear brother — the book is not a fake. I guess I shouldn't leave such forbidden books lying around. I'm sorry." He smirked.

"This is your doing! This chaos, the fake book! This disorder reeks of your tainted hand. I command you to show this room how Delirium taints your hand."

The room stood still, jarred at the thought of the *Kiss of Death* — *the Delirium* nearby.

The Darkest Night smugly rolled down his sleeve and bared his hand openly.

All gasped, nearly fainting at his hand marked by a bulging blue vein.

"Can everyone see that his hand is tainted by Delirium? It's all his doing — his plan to ruin the Sun. To impose his darkness! We need to release the Sun at once." Night ordered.

Calmly, the Darkest Night stood and smugly said, "Just one minute, dear brother, I showed you mine. Now you show me yours. Show everyone your ruling hand."

"Surely!" Said Night, but when he rolled up his sleeve, he became stunned to see the exact mark. The same blue vein ran in the precise spot of the Night's ruling hand.

The Darkest Night snickered. "Oh dear brother, Now everyone knows our dreadful family secret — our great grandmama's blue veins. Or, as I refer to it — the blue vein of my existence. It doesn't make our hands tainted. It just means bad genes run in our family. Luckily for us, our ruffled sleeves cover them right up."

All laughed in relief, but the Night grew silent. He didn't know what to make out of his brother's games, nor did he understand why he, the ruler of Night, wasn't being heard or taken seriously.

Then someone from the Sun's court yelled, "But what about the Sun? who will rise in the morning? She must be released! She must rise!"

The Head Council of Order rose and said, "There is no doubt the Sun, our Queen, will rise again. But as our duty, we must follow protocol and run a thorough investigation. The Sun will not rise tomorrow. Please plan accordingly."

As chaos broke, Gossip got excited just thinking of the headlines from her news to report.

Then the Head Council of Order asked, "Is there anyone from the Sun's court that can rise for the Sun tomorrow? Dawn, what about you?"

Dawn, beginning to yawn again in low energy, said, "Who me? Take over the full day and pull a double shift? Not very likely. What about Sunshine?"

Sunshine, who stood close to the Guards of Order, trying to get more information about the Sun's whereabouts, became flabbergasted at the suggestion. "Me? I'm the commander, head of security. I can't just leave my post. What about the Festival Goddesses of Light? I'm sure all of them together can handle such a task."

"Did I just manifest this?" wondered Lampetia quietly, in awe of her power.

Neera, the Festival Goddess of Light's sister, interrupted. "It's scary how quickly you're manifesting right now, Lampetia, but it's simply bad timing. Don't get us wrong, council, we would love to rise for the Sun, but it's festival season and the big ones are coming up. We can't make it."

"Alright then, does anyone have any suggestions?" asked the Council of Order.

The Darkest Night raised his finger. "May I suggest the Goddess of Desire?"

Night stomped his foot. "The Goddess of Desire is not of light, but of fire. The world will burn!"

Wanting the matter to be resolved quickly, the Council of Order considered the Darkest Night's suggestion and said, "In light of the most recent events, the Goddess of Desire has impressed us all with her radiance — her electricity. Do you think she is up for the task? And where is she now?"

The Darkest Night pointed towards the glass window. "She is now with the Moon, still casting her Ring of Fire onto the world."

Night slammed his fist and said, "Has everyone gone mad? I am king, the Night, standing tall before you all, telling you that the Goddess of Desire is not fit for such a role. Am I not being firm in my voice?"

The Head Council of Order replied to the Night. "Yes, my King, we hear you clearly, but you are too close to the situation and are losing your ability to think rationally and calmly. You are too biased to rule on the matter. I have to make the decision and until we get this sorted with the Sun Queen, I have decided the Goddess of Desire will rise for the Sun. Besides, the world can use some desire — some heat — some spice. If she can make the world feel the way she made us all feel today, the world might find itself in a better place. Is everyone in agreement with me? All in agreement say, 'hear ye, hear ye.' Yes?"

Thrown by the bombshell of events, on the Sun's very own Golden Jubilee, all stood looking at each other, dazed and not knowing what to think. But when they glanced out the glass window, the Ring of Fire blazed in alluring desire. One by one, until their voices aligned in unison, they exclaimed, "Hear ye! Hear ye!"

The Night dissipated into the vastness and snuck into the Tower chamber in search of the Sun. Lying in a pool of her golden tears, the Night found her. He sat by her side and morphed back into form. "My love, what has happened? Is it true? Did you attempt to read the book?"

She sat up and held him tightly. "I'm so ashamed. Yes, I read it, but even though I now carry the burden of shame, I don't have any regrets about what I did. I only wish you would have told me what I came to find out. Why didn't you tell me?"

The Night wiped the tears from the Sun's face and said, "My love, I should have told you that I didn't get to finish the book. I guess my own ego kept me from telling you, but I barely read it before it burned in a fire. I was shocked to see another version of the book, which is the one you read. What did you learn from the book that has you in this state?"

The Sun exhaled. "You were right to be concerned about your brother, but he is not the one to blame. Your brother is merely a host to the Delirium rose that pricked him. It will slowly grow strong in him as well in all of us. We will all become infected by it."

Night put his head down and rested it on her shoulder. "I had a suspicion it was growing in him. The rose pricked him as a child and since then, Mother and I have always watched him closely. It was our family secret that we kept hidden from the rest of the Mystical realm. He seemed to grow up fine, but tonight I witnessed the toying nature — the manipulation from the Delirium. He convinced both courts to put forth the Goddess of Desire to rise in your honor."

Aghast, the Sun rose. "The Goddess of Desire! Rise in my place? This is the start, isn't it? It is the beginning of the end."

The Night nodded his head in sadness. "Yes, and as the world slowly burns, she will burn with it. Her fate is grim. Brace yourself, my love; the Dark Ages will soon recycle themselves."

With desperation in her tone, the Sun asked, "And the rat? Your chosen one?"

"I'm not even sure if it's enough to stop what I fear is coming, but we can hope. The rat carries the Goddess of Desire's last whisper, which was the last thing I came to learn from the book. It said: *When the Fire Goddess kisses the Darkest of Nights, she will lose her gift of whisper and the world will only know of her fire.*"

The Sun paced the room, trying to find reason in it all. "So if your brother is the host of Delirium, then the rat will be the host of Hope."

The Night perked up to see the Sun radiating with a plan. "Yes. When the rat releases the Goddess of Desire's whisper by making its dream come true, we might have a chance to conquer the Delirium Rose."

"And the Greatest Wind? Where is he? I didn't see him at the Jubilee."

"Ah, yes, I cast him out for good reasons."

Appalled, the Sun asked, "Which are? We need him!"

"Well, one, let's just say he deserved such punishment and let's leave it at that. I also thought it best for him to be earthbound — a hard lesson to get a better perspective on Love. But now I feel it was the best decision. He can help us from that end — from Earth."

The Sun brightened once more. "Then let's not give up. I'll make sure on my end that the rat is protected. So the rat will have the Sun and the Night on its side!"

Then, clamoring footsteps disrupted them.

"My Good Night, you must leave before they find you here and lock you up too."

The Night bowed to the Sun and kissed her hand. "May this all be over soon, my love. Stay strong." Then vanished into his vast darkness.

The Forgotten Whisper

It was hard for Charlie to witness someone titled the Greatest Wind lose his might and dwindle into a heartbroken mess. His self-destruction began with the Storm Steep — Charlie had to keep an eye on it. Gaseous in its suds to boost mystic strength — the Storm Steep was only to be taken as a shot because of its fuel. Unfortunately, the Greatest Wind got in the habit of not only sneaking hard shots of it but guzzling it until his winds tail-spun into oblivion, which sent a gaseous sulfurous scent wafting into town. It alarmed the human townspeople, who began investigating the mysteriously potent smell.

Dwight, a southern mystic, walked into *Desiree's Tavern*, standoffish and clasping his nose tightly with a clothespin. "Alright, where is he, Charlie? Where's that son of a gun — Greatest Gassy Wind is what he should be called. Coming to town and putting us all in jeopardy. Where is he?"

Charlie collected all the Storm Steep bottles from the saloon shelves. "Calm down, Dwight. He's just been letting off some steam. He's out cold in the back and in pretty rough shape. So give him a break."

"Really? Just letting off some steam, is he? Do you see this clothespin gnawing at my nose, Charlie? I swear I can light a match and this entire state will blow to bits. You need to control that Greatest Gassy Wind before the human townspeople start their witch hunt and come knocking on this door! Or, more importantly, mine!"

"Don't worry. I've got it under control. It'll be fine. Go home, Dwight!"

"I can't go home with this stank in the air. I now have to go knocking on Rosie's portal, way out west, and see if she'll take me in! You know I don't like going back there to her. So you better take care of this!" Dwight sneeringly pointed his finger as he sputtered off.

Charlie sighed and nodded in disbelief when he stepped into the brew hanger and saw the Greatest Wind conked out under the dripping Storm Steep brew nozzle. "Ah no! Come on Greatest! You *are* gonna blow us to bits. I'm pulling the plug on this NOW." Charlie flipped the switch and shut off all Storm Steep brewing.

Charlie pulled and dragged at the Greatest Wind's billows, trying to get him to bed, slightly waking him up from his zombie state.

Slurring in his words, the Greatest Wind announced, "Love sucketh, Charlie. It wrangled me like a clown to a rodeo and now look at me. Fallen! Disgraced! While she's with that piece of no good Night Darkness. I knew opening my heart to Love wasn't a good idea, and now I can't seem to close it. I opened up Pandora's box!"

"Come on now, Greatest, you gotta keep that Love strong. Don't let it drag you down. Speaking of dragging, can you help me get you to bed?" Grappling at the Greatest Wind's billows with one shoulder under him. Then he noticed the Greatest Wind conked out cold. "Alright, I guess not."

When Charlie finally got the Greatest Wind safely to his Tempur-pedic cloud. He looked down on him with concern, "Tomorrow is a new day, Greatest. I hope you find peace when you can't find a single drop of that Storm Steep."

But little did Charlie know, this would begin Act II of the Greatest Wind's broken heart saga — the Rain. Sappy tears fell nonstop and were flooding the Texas town.

Dwight stepped into *Desiree's Tavern*, wringing himself like a sopping mop. "Where is he, Charlie? We need to send that doggone Wind back to Night's court NOW! He's killing our crops!"

"Now, now, Dwight, A little rain is always a good thing during this dry season," said Charlie as he placed a bucket under the leaking roof."

Dwight stomped in his slush. "A little rain? Never mind my crops, but my precious dandelions are as good as dead. My dandelions, Charlie! What's wrong with him anyways?"

Charlie leaned into Dwight and said in a hushed tone, "Alright, I'll tell you, cause you, out of everyone, should understand. The Greatest Wind has a situation. Well, to explain it best… It's like your situation with Rosie."

Dwight became squeamish at the mere mention of it. "Ohhhhh, matters of the heart, that ain't good for no one around here. I'm not sticking around for this mess, but Charlie, I'll tell you what, you best clean it up before he becomes reckless, like I was."

Charlie knew he needed to intervene before the Greatest Wind caused a natural disaster, but he didn't know how to since the Greatest Wind kept sulking in his rain, not saying a single word.

Charlie stepped outside the saloon to find two renegade Dark Clouds motoring off the skyway and pulling up to the Greatest Wind.

"Compadre, what you need is some good old-fashioned hurricane fun — eye of the storm type of trouble," advised Lowel, keeping his motor running. "That will make you bounce back and get you out of this rut."

Rosie trailed in, revving smoky gray patches of puff through the sky. "Or join us! We're heading to Mexico for beach rays and tropical storms, which helped me get over Dwight. Yup, a good storm and a power ballad wiped the slate clean, alright."

The Greatest Wind stood silent, gesturing with slight smirks and head nods to be polite.

Lowel noticed Charlie heading towards them. "Oh, here he comes, the no-fun police." Then with a head tilt and a change of tone: "Why hello there, Charlie."

Charlie tipped his cowboy hat. "Lowel, Rosie, what brings you this way? Hopefully not trouble."

"No need to worry about us, Charlie; we're just passing through, heading south of the border. We heard our good commander, my compadre here, was in town. So we thought we would pay our respects." Said Lowel.

"Yeah, we're trying to convince him to come with us to Mexico." Said Rosie.

Charlie turned to the Greatest Wind. "Before you decide on anything. I do need some help tending to the bar. Remember, you asked me if I needed any help. Well, I certainly can use it."

The Greatest Wind side-eyed Charlie and finally spoke. "I'm a wind of my word. Fine, I'll get to work." Then gave Lowel and Roise a half-salute and walked back into the tavern.

Frustrated, Charlie tossed the Greatest Wind a cleaning rag. "Okay, it's time to lift the rain. I've been your caretaker — cleaning your mess around town, and I didn't want to say anything because it's obvious you're going through some heartache, but you're stirring up a mess in this town. So if you plan on staying, I suggest you finally get to work. Do you even want to work here or are you passing the time?"

It was the push the Greatest Wind needed. He realized his actions had been selfish and didn't want to lose Charlie as a friend. So he lifted his rain and said, "You're a good man, Charlie. Thank you for taking me in, your right; work can do me some good. I think I've dried out anyway."

Charlie poured a glass of Moon's Milk, soothing to the billows after rain, and slid it across the bar to him. "You know the one thing humans got right about time is their saying, *Time heals all wounds*. I think that's just what you need — time and this town's got plenty of it."

"How do you know so much about Time, Charlie?" The Greatest Wind asked, guzzling Moon's milk.

Charlie quickly buttoned up and handed him a crate of pint glasses. "It's time you get to work and help me shine some glasses for tonight's crew."

Soon after, word got out that the Greatest Wind was the new barkeep at *Desiree's Tavern*, which attracted wind business. High Winds, Low Winds, Gusts, Land Breezes, Valley Winds, Trade Winds and Locals of all sorts stopped by the tavern to salute their commander and get advice on air pressure, which was something the Greatest Wind had mastered. It was a nice change to be so close to his troops, who didn't see him as Fallen but as their commander and teacher. Charlie was right; all the Greatest Wind needed was Time and it was ticking well for the Greatest Wind and even for Charlie.

One day, when tending the bar, Joan walked in. Charlie could sense by the brassy luster in her eye that she was a time traveler.

"Are you Charlie?" She asked with a bright smile.

Charlie became weary and answered abrasively. "Why do you want to know?"

She leaned in over the bar and whispered. "It's okay. Your secret is safe with me. Your parents sent me."

Charlie cautiously looked around the bar and noticed Joan was drawing attention with her good looks. He turned to the Greatest Wind and said, "I'm taking my break. Do you mind taking over?"

The Greatest Wind had never seen Charlie's face blush and turn so blotchy, but he dismissed it when he saw Joan trying to get Charlie's attention. He smirked. "Sure, take as long as you want."

Charlie went outside and Joan followed.

When Charlie got far enough from the bar, he turned to her and scuffed, "Who are you? And What do you want?"

"Hi, I'm Joan. I'm also a Warper. You don't have to worry about me though. Your parents said you could help me settle. I've spent my whole life in the maze. I can't tell you if I'm in the past, future or the present. All I know is that I want to be still and just be. Can you help me settle?"

Charlie didn't know what to make of Joan or if he could trust her, so he firmly said. "Look, nobody here knows that I'm a Warper. They just see me as Charlie, the mystic barkeep, and I would like to keep it that way."

"That sounds lovely to be something other than a Warper. Can you help me be something? Please." Implored Joan with a sweet squint in her eye.

Charlie mulled it over for a second and forewarned her. "Look, mystics aren't too kind to 'Time Thieves' as most refer to us. If you want to settle, you have to get used to not being a Warper. That means no time travel and no jumping on any trains. Your identity and especially mine are top secret. Nobody can know. Are you certain you can live that way?"

"I wouldn't be here if I wasn't certain of this and I don't think your parents would have led me to you if they didn't trust me. They love you and want me to tell you that over and over. They even wanted me to hug you for them, but I don't think it's appropriate."

Charlie tried to shake off getting emotional over his parents. He missed them and Joan was right; they wouldn't send her if they had the slightest suspicions of bad intentions. So he grabbed her duffle bag and said, "Alright, there is a trailer in the back where you can stay until you get settled."

With a screeching yell of excitement, she hugged Charlie. "Thank you! Thank you! Thank you!"

Little by little, a friendship began to blossom between Charlie and Joan and in warping speed, it led to Love. Charlie was the happiest he had ever been and increasingly began to spend more time with Joan and less time at the tavern.

"What are you and Joan up to tonight?" said the Greatest Wind while wiping pint glasses and restocking shelves.

After straightening his collar in the mirror, Charlie said, "The State Fair just opened up, and I thought I would take Joan there. It seems like it would be fun. Have you ever been?"

The Greatest Wind flinched at the mention of the Texas State Fair, which triggered his memory of — her. "Yup, been there."

Charlie noticed the distaste of the subject for the Greatest Wind, so he shrugged it off and said, "OK. Will you be alright tending the bar yourself?"

"Yup. It'll be a slow night anyway."

But when the Greatest Wind unlocked the portal to open *Desiree's Tavern*, to his surprise, the parking lot was full of mystic bandits. The Howling Winds swept right into the tavern, known for their eerie sound. They liked to break glass with their high pitch frequency and scare the bejeezus out of anyone who crossed their paths. The Lone Stars scattered themselves at their usual spots. They were fixtures at the tavern, mysterious in their ways, and sat quietly hovering over their pints unless they were crossed. Then, it would be a mutiny for all. The Time Thieves appeared from somewhere amid time and plopped themselves right at a table. Everyone always watched them, not knowing if they were changing or thieving the time.

There was one instance at the tavern when they held time frozen. When time adjusted again, patrons of the tavern found themselves unclothed and free of their possessions. It took a while after that for Charlie to let them back inside the saloon, and a watchful eye kept them in check. Then Dwight, a mystic farmer, agriculturalist to all southern mystics, stomped in with his crop-crusader buddies. Dwight wasn't a rebel nor a bandit and usually had good intentions, but his mouth usually ran itself to a scuffle. Finally, all situated themselves, ready to refuel their bandit supernatural powers.

It was a nice distraction for the Greatest Wind to be on his billowing toes, busy, and not thinking of — her, especially on a Texas State Fair night, which reminded him of her fire. A fire that blazed in rings streaking the roller coaster on that fateful night — he pinned it to the moment he knew he loved her.

"Hey Greatest, you're outta Witches' Brew. Can we get some from the back?" Dwight hung over the bar, messing with the brew nozzle.

The Greatest Wind snapped his cleaning rag at him. "Get on your side of the fence, Dwight! Besides, we don't carry anything called Witches' Brew."

"You carry it, but I don't call it by its real name," Dwight said, opening his eyes widely as if speaking telepathically.

The Greatest Wind winced at the odd expression and then thought of the label he was referring to — *Ah, Rosie's brew!* Then he smirked. "Alright, I think I can get some from the back if you mind the bar."

"I am your Captain." He saluted. "Try to get a crate of it!"

Just as the Greatest Wind lifted a crate full of Rosie's Brew, the slump of Maestro's mystic box shape, taped in bubble wrap, caught his eye. He dropped the crate, jumped over the roped barricade, and cautiously unwrapped Maestro. A minute or two went by and he stood gawking at it. He weighed out the consequences of inserting the quarter he held in his hand, but none mattered. He needed to tell her how he felt once and for all. The rush of spontaneity filled him with hope, so he plugged Maestro right into the socket and tossed the quarter heads first into its mouth.

He waited for Maestro's lights to turn on, but they didn't. "Come on, Maestro! You came alive before. You have to let me see her!" Then he began to shake Maestro. "Turn on! Turn on! Turn on! I say!" He pounded on the console. Then he pleaded. "Maestro, I just want to tell her that I love her. I was such a fool to push her away and fight against great Joy, Love, and…."

He slumped to his knees in the agony of the thought. "Destiny. I can't help thinking that if I had been there, maybe our Destiny would have seen the light of the Sun and Night. Of course, it's all my fault. But, please, just let me make it right, Maestro."

Maestro didn't light up nor give any flickering indication that it wanted to turn on. After minutes passed, the Greatest Wind stood up, dusted himself off and took it in stride. He was now getting used to the hard-luck life of being Fallen. He strapped Rosie's brew on his back and brought it to the front of the tavern.

Rosie's Brew wasn't like any other brews made to fuel a mystic with power. Instead, Rosie's Brew fueled mystics with life's journey. "It's the perfect brew because there's no such thing as too much of it." So Rosie would say to the Greatest Wind upon delivery.

The Greatest Wind slammed a pint of it and was now going to test her theory. So he sat down with the Howling Winds and entered into Act III of his broken heart — Recklessness.

The bar was in shambles. The Greatest Wind let the bandits run amuck while he took part of it. "Rosie said a good power ballad helped her wipe the slate clean, so if it worked for good old Rosie, then maybe it'll work for me too." He said this to a Howling Wind that handed him a microphone. The Greatest Wind then stood on stage and piped the best he could to a karaoke power ballad: it was all fun at first. Some bandits joined in; some took out their lighters and began to sway. But something about the song unleashed the last bit of hurt brewing in his winds. Feeling

THE NIGHT'S FABLE

forgotten by Night, the court, the Goddess of Desire, and now Maestro, he belted out the forbidden howl of a thousand winds. It signified the end. Every window in town shuddered in its haunting frequency. Dwight stood, cockeyed and brain scrambled from the menacing pitch, then flat out dropped like a fly. The rest of the bandits quickly fled, plugging their ears with anything they could find.

After his musical debut, the Greatest Wind looked around to find himself alone. "Fine! Just leave me like everyone else!" He sulked. Then he stumbled on Dwight in his stupor. "Oops, didn't see you there Dwight. Thanks for sticking around." He propped Dwight's unconscious body on a chair and grabbed more brew. He guzzled it until he was full of life's journey.

Finally, he slumped and laid his head onto the bar table while his eyelids became heavy and shut in the final curtain call. He willingly closed his eyes — never wanting to wake.

What the Greatest Wind wasn't aware of was that he wasn't forgotten, at least not by the whisper that was. Such a forgotten whisper, unrecorded and undetected by even the Goddess of Desire that created it — let it drift into a fanning air without a Low Wind to carry. It must have been the throes of her pain in labor with Destiny that made her forget about it. The whisper, though, didn't forget and it didn't forget its recipient — the Greatest Wind.

"Wheee!" said the forgotten whisper, with a fierce spirit that went on a journey — a life's journey to fulfill its purpose. "Wheee!" Exclaimed the forgotten whisper that learned when to float, when to descend and when to ride. "Wheee!" It shouted to the world when it discovered how to hitchhike its way with welcoming birds that helped it along. From the highest mountain peaks to the city streets, "Wheee! Wheee! Wheee!" said the forgotten whisper that grew stronger every day, in every way.

Like a Viking, it saddled itself on eagles that glided through the skies. It slid off the arches of rainbows; it vaulted itself off lightning and swung off the trapeze of branches and streetlights. Its determination only got more robust even with its setbacks. "Wheee!" Cried the forgotten whisper that nearly caught the Greatest Wind's ear at the West Village park but missed and then couldn't catch up to his speed. "Wheee!" Cheered the forgotten whisper that finally made it back to Shiner, full circle, where its journey began and where the Greatest Wind was, at last, perfectly still.

The forgotten whisper descended like a parachuter and aimed itself to land at *Desiree's Tavern*. It floated right in through the broken glass window and then landed on the bar, where it jumped and airlifted itself into a series of backflips from one bar stool to the other until it got near the Greatest Winds ear. Then, like a ninja, it floated swiftly about to enter the Greatest Wind's ear. "Whee!" It shouted with glee. Until the Greatest Wind released a strong spouting puff of wind that sent the whisper tumbling back a few feet to the ground.

The whisper shook itself from the sharp blow and, with a ferocious yell, went charging towards the Greatest Wind with a toothpick and a stir straw. "Ayyy!" It exclaimed as it vaulted itself from Dwight's unconscious limp body onto the Frigidaire air conditioning window unit. There it waited until the cold air kicked in, then made its next move and swung like Tarzan from the streamers that flapped from the dusty vent. Once in mid-air, it somersaulted and floated right above the Greatest Wind's funneling target of an ear. The forgotten whisper took a moment to reflect on its journey and how far it had come and then roared, "Wheee!" as it swan dove right in.

It drilled through his eardrum, filled with Resentment and Anger, then sawed through the barbed wire billows of Bitterness, and once it excavated through the Sadness and Guilt that remained, it made its way to his heart. Rather than ignite a spirit like any of the typical Goddess of Desire's whispers — the forgotten whisper detonated it.

The town shook in waves as the Greatest Wind convulsed in the throes of the throbbing and burning whisper. Stumbling and crawling out of the tavern and onto his knees, the Greatest Wind looked to Night's sky, where the Goddess of Desire emerged, striking her flames that ran in her Ring of Fire — just like it ran with him at the State Fair. Such an eclipse of Desire activated the whisper, filling his winds with an inferno of fiery speed. He closed his eyes, stinging in hot tears while his billows furiously pounded at the ground with scorching flames. He then heard Destiny's childlike voice ringing in his ear. "Daddy, I am with you. Destiny is on your side."

He would no longer be bound by duty or the glory of a title, but bound by a new sense of purpose — one with relentless, unfearing, unwavering — Love. Just as the pain subsided and he watched the Goddess of Desire's torching eclipse from a world away, he knew it wasn't over.

It all had just begun.

CPSIA information can be obtained
at www.ICGtesting.com
Printed in the USA
JSHW052101091222
34347JS00002B/120